SUPERIOR INTRIGUE

MICHAEL CARRIER

A number of very wonderful people helped me prepare this book for publication. Each of them contributed significantly.

Thank you Evie, Meredith, and Charity.

Thank you Steve W., Jeff K., and Jim M. for reviewing my treatment of firearms.

And special thanks always to George and Gay.

SUPERIOR

INTRIGUE

MICHAEL CARRIER

GREENWICH VILLAGE INK

GRAND RAPIDS, MICHIGAN

SUPERIOR INTRIGUE

Published 2014 by Greenwich Village Ink, Grand Rapids, MI.

Visit the JACK website at http://www.greenwichvillageink.com/
For additional information (and sometimes puzzles) visit JACK's blog: http://jackhandlerny.blogspot.com/.

Author can be emailed at mike.jon.carrier@gmail.com. You can follow Michael's tweets at @MikeCarrier999.

ISBN: 978-1-936092-29-1 (trade pbk)
Printed in the United States of America

Library of Congress Cataloging-in-Publication Data

Carrier, Michael.
SUPERIOR INTRIGUE / by Michael Carrier. 1st ed.
ISBN: 978-1-936092-29-1 (trade pbk. : alk. paper)
1. Hard Boiled Thriller 2. Mystery 3. Thriller 4. Novel 5. Murder 6. Burglary. 7. New York. 8. Michigan's Upper Peninsula.

Contents

What people are saying about the "Getting to Know Jack" series

Finally, there is a new author who will challenge the likes of Michael Connelly and David Baldacci. — Island Books

If you like James Patterson and Michael Connelly, you'll love Michael Carrier. Carrier has proven that he can hang with the best of them. It has all of the great, edge-of-your-seat action and suspense that you'd expect in a good thriller, and it kept me guessing to the very end. Fantastic read with an awesome detective duo—I couldn't put it down! — Katie

Don't read Carrier at the beach or you are sure to get sunburned. I did. I loved the characters. It was so descriptive you feel like you know everyone. Lots of action—always something happening. I love the surprise twists. All my friends are reading it now because I wouldn't talk to them until I finished it so they knew it was good. Carrier is my new favorite author! — Sue

Thoroughly enjoyed this read — kept me turning page after page! Good character development and captivating plot. Had theories but couldn't quite solve the mystery without reading to the end. Highly recommended for readers of all ages. — Terry

Top Shelf Murder Mystery—Riveting. Being a Murder-Mystery "JUNKIE" this book is definitely a keeper ... can't put it down ... read it again type of book...and it is very precise to the lifestyles in Upper Michigan. Very well researched. I am a resident of this area. His attention to detail is great. I have to rate this book in the same class or better than authors Michael Connelly, James Patterson and Steve Hamilton. — Shelldrakeshores

Being a Michigan native, I was immediately drawn to this book. Michael Carrier is right in step with his contemporaries James Patterson and David Baldacci. I am anxious to read more of his work. I highly recommend this one! — J. Henningsen

A fast and interesting read. Michael ends each chapter with a hook that makes you want to keep reading. The relationship between father and daughter is compelling. Good book for those who like a quick moving detective story where the characters often break the "rules" for the greater good! I'm looking forward to reading the author's next book. — Flower Lady

Move over Patterson, I now have a new favorite author, Jack and his daughter make a great tag team, great intrigue, and diversions. I have a cabin on Sugar Island and enjoyed the references to the locations. I met the author at Joey's coffee shop up on the hill, (the real live Joey) great writer, good stuff. I don't usually finish a book in the course of a week, but read this one in two sittings so it definitely had my attention. I am looking forward to the next installment. Bravo. — Northland Press

My husband is not a reader— he probably hasn't read a book since his last elementary school book report was due. But ... he took my copy of Murder on Sugar Island to deer camp and read the whole thing in two days. After he recommended the book to me, I read it— being the book snob that I am, I thought I had the whole plot figured out within the first few pages, but a few chapters later, I was mystified once again. After that surprise ending, we ordered the other two Getting to Know Jack books. — Erin W.

I enjoyed this book very much. It was very entertaining, and the story unfolded in a believable manner. Jack Handler is a likable character. But you would not like to be on his wrong side. Handler made that very clear in Jack and the New York Death Mask. This book (Murder on Sugar Island) was the first book in the Getting to Know Jack series that I read. After I read Death Mask, I discovered just how tough Jack Handler really was.

I heard that Carrier is about to come out with another Jack Handler book—a sequel to Superior Peril. I will read it the day it becomes available. And I will undoubtedly finish it before I go to bed. If he could write them faster, I would be happy.

Actually, I'll take what I can get. — Deborah M.

I thoroughly enjoyed this book. I could not turn the pages fast enough. I am not sure it was plausible, but I love the characters. I highly recommend this book and look forward to reading more by Michael Carrier. — Amazon Reader

An intense thrill ride!! — Mario

Michael Carrier has knocked it out of the park — John

Left on the edge of my seat after the last book, I could not wait for the next chapter to unfold and Mike Carrier did not disappoint! I truly feel I know his characters better with each novel and I especially like the can-do/will-do attitude of Jack. Keep up the fine work, Mike and may your pen never run dry! — SW

The Handlers are at it again, with the action starting on Sugar Island, I am really starting to enjoy the way the father daughter and now Red are working through the mind of Mike Carrier. The entire family, plus a few more are becoming the reason for the new sheriff's increased body count and antacid intake. The twists and turns we have come to expect are all there and then some. I'm looking for the next installment already. — Northland Press

Preface

If you enjoy this book you should consider writing a short review on Amazon after reading it. (http://amzn.to/1jvjNSi).

If you would like to learn a little more about the hows and the whys of writing Amazon reviews, please visit this site: http://www.greenwichvillageink.com/reviews.htm. It will be greatly appreciated.

SUPERIOR INTRIGUE (INTRIGUE) is the fourth part of the "Getting to Know Jack" series. All books in the series are available in print through Amazon and select bookstores, and all are available as eBooks through the Amazon Kindle Bookstore.

The first book of the series is entitled *JACK AND THE NEW YORK DEATH MASK (JACK)*. Two of the three main characters of the series (Jack and Kate Handler) were introduced in *JACK*.

MURDER ON SUGAR ISLAND (SUGAR) is part two of the "Getting to Know Jack" series.

SUPERIOR PERIL (PERIL) is the third book of the series.

INTRIGUE picks up where *PERIL* leaves off. In this book Jack, Kate, Red and Robby work at solving the murders of Robby's parents.

A longer backstory is provided in the Cast of Characters section at the end of this book.

For additional information visit Jack's page on the publisher's website at: http://www.greenwichvillageink.com/.

The author, Michael Carrier, holds a Master of Arts degree

from New York University, and has worked in private security for over two decades.

DISCLAIMER: None of the books in the "Getting to Know Jack" series represent true stores—they are all works of fiction. All characters, names, situations and occurrences are purely the product of the author's imagination. Any resemblance to actual events, or persons (living or dead), is totally coincidental.

Chapter 1

The catfight

(A short back-story is included in the "Cast of Characters" section at the end of this book)

"Do you remember how to get off this island?" Festerman asked his associate, David Nacow.

"Not exactly," Nacow replied as their rented Suburban wound its way along a gravel road. "This doesn't look familiar. Probably should have paid more attention on our way in. But, hell, it's such a *small* island. We're probably okay."

"See what you can do with the GPS," Festerman suggested.

"If we were in my car, I'd have no problem. I'll take a look."

"No need," Festerman interrupted as he slowed down. "I recognize *this* road. If I turn left here, it'll take us straight to the ferry road."

Nacow was pleased by those words. He was having a difficult time figuring out how to use the rental's Garmin.

Neither man spoke again until after the ferry attendant had directed them into the front position of lane two.

"Lights off," Nacow chuckled, reading the posted instructions. "They want you to turn your lights off. Like it's gonna make a difference."

Festerman fiddled around with the switch until he got the headlights turned off. He did leave the engine running.

A black Jeep that had been behind them pulled into lane three—directly even with Nacow's door. He glanced over as it came to a stop.

It was driven by a very attractive Marilyn Monroe blonde—bright blue eyes, full red lips, delicious smile, and tight red sweater.

She acknowledged his attention with her eyes.

As he flirted with the blonde, a second young woman leaned forward to get a good look at him. When her eyes met Nacow's she flashed a salacious smile and gave him a finger wiggle wave. Most likely in her early twenties, she appeared to be seven to ten years younger than the blonde. Nacow was even more impressed by the passenger.

"Wow! Look at the muscles on that girl. I'm joining *her* gym."

The younger girl, a stunning redhead, flaunted a green camisole that not only enhanced the striking hue of her green eyes but also showed off her well-developed upper body strength.

"This is strictly a business trip," the older man said in a fatherly voice. "We're not window shopping."

"I know, but it never hurts to see what's out there."

"For all we know they work at Jack's resort. And we'll end up running into them tomorrow. It is, after all, a *very* small island."

"I understand," Nacow said, stealing one more glance at the girls parked next to them. Then, with a big smile on his face, he closed his eyes and lay back on the headrest.

"What the *hell* is goin' on!" Festerman blurted out.

The blonde had opened her door and stepped out onto the deck of the ferry.

"You bitch!" she screamed loudly, using both hands to slam her door. She then ran around in front of her vehicle to get at the passenger.

Both Festerman and Nacow watched intently.

By the time the blonde reached the other side of her car, the redhead had already jumped out, slamming her door with equal animation.

The blonde clutched the younger girl by the hair and slapped her—not once but several times.

"You're nothin' but a cheap whore!" the blonde screamed. "I *knew* you couldn't be trusted."

The young redhead tried pushing the blonde woman off, kicking her fiercely on the shins several times with her cowboy boots.

"*You're* the slut!" the redhead shouted back through her tears. "That's right! You heard me! You might be my sister, but you're nothin' but a slut. You don't deserve him! You sleep around with any guy that'll have you. He deserves better than you. S-L-U-T! That's what you are. And you *know* it. Hell! *Everybody* knows it. It's no secret."

Fearing the blonde was about to throw a punch with her free hand, the redhead grabbed it. So the blonde released her sister's hair and drew her hand back into a fist.

Seeing her chance, the redhead turned and darted toward the back of the ferry, screaming over her shoulder as she ran.

Festerman and Nacow turned in their seats to watch, as did most of the other passengers on the ferry.

Bill, the Sugar Island Ferry attendant on duty, jumped between the sisters just as they reached the railing.

"Ladies, this has to stop! Right *now*! Relax. Calm down. Or I'll have to get the cops to meet us on the Soo side."

"*She* picked the fight," the redhead said to Bill, while still trying to stare down her sister.

"You heard what he said, bitch," the blonde retorted. "If you don't shut up he's gonna have *you* arrested. Now get your ass back in the car and shut up. Or you can walk back. Can you do that? Can you shut up?"

As the girls were arguing, a man dressed in a long black coat, baseball cap, and sunglasses quietly slid out of the passenger side of the car directly behind Festerman and Nacow. Carrying a woolen blanket draped over his right arm, he walked up and tapped on Festerman's window. Smiling, he motioned for Festerman to lower it. Harold complied.

"You're Harold Festerman, right?"

Harold smiled and replied, "I am. But who are you?"

Nacow was still totally engrossed in the catfight behind him, so he never turned around to check out their visitor.

Pop.

Nacow heard but did not recognize the sound of a suppressed .22 caliber Long Rifle round. He did, however, notice the spray of warm red liquid that had showered him. And he sensed a slight thud striking his left torso.

The shooter had aimed the pistol so that the bullet would pierce both sides of Festerman's brain. By establishing a slightly downward trajectory, he also assured himself that the bullet would strike Nacow's torso just in back of his left elbow and lodge in his lung.

The shooter had chosen .22 caliber Long Rifle rounds, with full metal jackets, because he knew that they would sustain sufficient velocity and not be deflected by the victim's skull. Plus, the metal jacket minimized the size of the exit wound, thus reducing blood spatter.

Reaching far into the vehicle with a fully extended right arm, the shooter fired his next round. The bullet passed through Nacow's head and struck the stanchion between the front and rear doors.

Confident that both men were dead or dying, he snatched the loose material of Festerman's right trouser leg and pulled his foot off of the accelerator. The involuntary tightening of muscles had caused the driver to crush down on the gas pedal as he was dying.

The shooter then fired one additional round in each of the victims.

Because of the enormous commotion continuing between the two beautiful girls at the rear of the ferry, no one noticed the killer opening the driver's door, unhooking Festerman's seatbelt, and shoving his body to the floor in front of Nacow.

The killer then sat down behind the wheel, shut the door, and spread the blanket over Festerman's body.

Analyzing Nacow's posture, with head tilted backward as though sleeping, the killer casually reached over and closed the dead man's eyes. He then checked to be sure his seatbelt was fastened.

When the two women observed the brake lights on the car parked beside theirs flash several times, they immediately stopped shouting.

"Look," the younger sister said, feigning reconciliation. "If you're willing to drop it, so am I. Whaddya think? Shall we forget it for now? I don't want trouble with the law."

The blonde threw her arms around her rival and hugged her. Holding hands and smiling, they squeezed their way between parked cars toward the front of the ferry and their Jeep. The drivers and passengers in half a dozen vehicles along the way began applauding.

Satisfied that the blood-spattered passenger window remained the only visible evidence of carnage, the killer rolled the window down and gave a thumbs-up to the blonde driver across from him as she settled into her Jeep.

Chapter 2

Earlier in the day

Even before entering her suite at the resort, Kate detected the aroma of whitefish fillets wafting out through the open kitchen window. Jack was preparing his favorite recipe.

Kate had spent most of the summer at the resort. She'd hoped for a relaxing two and a half months. But it didn't turn out that way—at least not so far.

She had requested and received a leave of absence from her job in New York.

Captain Spencer, who headed up the homicide detectives in her precinct, appreciated all the hardships she had experienced over the past year. As if taking a bullet in the line of duty weren't enough, when her uncle was shot to death at the same resort where she and her father were now staying, Captain Spencer decided to give her every opportunity possible to heal.

Besides, he was getting ready to retire, so he really didn't concern himself about how things looked. He figured that Kate would get everything settled and return to work in September, and then he'd retire.

Of course, he intended to promote her to lieutenant before his departure. Kate was his handpicked protégée.

Alex Garos, Kate's uncle, had named her in his will to inherit the Sugar Island resort. When Kate and her father, Jack Handler, a retired Chicago homicide detective, drove up from his home in Chicago to sign the inheritance papers, they became absorbed in solving her uncle's murder.

Once she and her father had unscrambled that crime, they found that she was inheriting more than just a resort. Her uncle had fathered a child from an illicit affair with his married female assistant. The boy, now fourteen, five years before Alex died, had suffered the loss of his mother and her husband in a house fire.

Alex tried to adopt the orphaned boy, but the county would not allow it. They determined that foster care would better suit the boy's needs than being raised by a single man who ran a resort, especially since that resort contained a bar.

The boy would have nothing to do with foster care, so after numerous attempts to place him, the county just gave up. As a result, the boy ended up living in the woods on his own and unofficially working odd jobs for Alex at the resort.

So, in addition to inheriting the resort, Kate became the legal guardian for the redheaded boy whom everyone referred to simply as Red—a name the child came by for obvious reasons.

No one even knew his real name. Red had been delivered by his legal father at home, without benefit of doctor or midwife. And, as is sometimes the case in rural America, such births never make it to county records. Therefore, as far as anyone knew, the name of the boy who spent most of his time with Alex Garos was simply *Red*—no middle name and no last name.

To add to the confusion, even if Red had known his last name he would not have been able to say so. His voice box had been injured several years earlier, and he was not physically capable of uttering an intelligible word. Up until Kate introduced him to a smartphone and the glories of texting, his ability to communicate had been limited to a variety of grunts and hand gestures.

In spite of this handicap, Red did have several things going for him. For one, he enjoyed the unconditional support of Jack and Kate. Not since his mother and her husband had passed away had Red been able to live with people who loved him.

Primarily that is what Kate brought to the relationship. At times she regarded him as the little brother she never had. And because she was old enough to be Red's mother, she frequently regarded her role in his life as just that—his mother.

Jack's part was multifaceted. Not only was he the closest thing to a real father figure Red had enjoyed in many years, but the boy also looked to Jack as a force to be reckoned with—one that was supremely powerful—at times larger than life and somewhat scary. But to Red, Jack was always supremely benevolent. Sort of like the Darth Vader of the prequel trilogy—an aura shared also by the Sugar Island community as a whole.

One of the other things about Red that worked in his favor was his pleasant countenance. He was a good-looking boy—his round freckled face framed by rings of soft red curls gave him the appearance of an angel. He would always give eye contact and a smile when communicating. Perhaps it was because of his inability to verbally communicate that he learned the power of eye contact and a big smile.

When Kate became Red's legal guardian she enrolled him in school in the Soo. While he did adjust willingly to this new experience, it did present for him one substantial challenge. During his first month, he was suspended three times for fighting.

Neither Jack nor Kate had expected that from Red. Prior to his having attended school all they had seen was a cheerful young man with a self-effacing sense of humor. And that's how he behaved in school. It was just that when a bully picked on him, Red would stand up for himself. And if need be, he would mix it up with anyone. The surprising part was that the result was always the same.

He was so quick and agile that, when the situation warranted, Red would dodge a first blow and then squarely land three of his own. When the confrontation was over, Red would still be smiling as he helped the other kid up.

All three times, both Jack and Kate were called down to the school to meet with Principal Hardigan. And in all instances, Jack's end of the conversation went something like this:

"Did Red start the fight? Did Red try to avoid the fight? Did Red throw the first punch?"

After the principal answered Jack's questions in Red's favor, Jack would then say, "Then Red wasn't really fighting—he was merely ducking and defending."

In the end Principal Hardigan would begrudgingly re-admit Red.

Fortunately, after the first month of school, the bullies stopped picking on Red.

It was those same characteristics, Red's resourcefulness and quiet resolve, that brought him into contact with Robby earlier that summer at Maritime Camp.

A bully had singled Robby out. Boxing his victim into a corner in a restroom, the young thug and two of his friends tried to shake Robby down for candy money. Red walked in at just the right time and put the bully on his rear end—three times. *Bang, bang, bang.*

The two boys immediately became best friends. They were a perfect match—Robby for his communication skills and native intelligence, and Red for the reasons mentioned above. When the two of them teamed up they became a formidable force at camp. No one wanted to deal with Robby's guile nor Red's lightning-fast punches.

While they were almost exactly the same age, they differed significantly in both physical appearance and personality. Robby had dark brown hair and eyes, which he had inherited from his father—Titus Gordon.

Red's red hair and inability to talk pretty much defined him.

Robby, like Red, was at that awkward age where the growth spurts sprouted long arms and even longer legs. Both boys jumped two sizes over the course of the summer, with Robby catching and slightly surpassing Red's five feet seven inches.

Chapter 3
The tragedy

It was during that summer, when both Red and Robby were fourteen years of age, that multiple tragedies turned Robby's life upside down.

It all started when Robby's mother came a day early to pull him out of summer camp. There was no warning—the head counselor just came over to where the two boys were playing and informed Robby that his mother was there to pick him up. After Robby and his mother had left, that same counselor gathered all the boys together and announced that a boat piloted by Robby's father, Titus Gordon, had gone missing on Lake Superior. Red was devastated.

But, the news got even worse.

The next day the car Robby and his mother were riding in was destroyed by a bomb. The blast killed his mother instantly, and severely injured him.

Adding to the tragedy of losing his mother, the same day his mother was killed he found himself kidnapped by an organized group of Russian gold thieves operating out of New York. The Russians, who had learned that Robby's father had discovered a Bronze Age shipwreck in Lake Superior and that he had salvaged numerous gold ingots from it, believed that Robby might know where his father had hidden the gold. They had kidnapped Robby in the hope that they could make him talk.

And then, making matters even worse, Robby was told that his father had succumbed to torture administered by the Russians in an effort to extract information regarding the location of the gold.

The bottom line—Robby learned about the murder of both of his parents within a forty-hour period.

While Jack and Kate were able to solve the case involving the kidnapping and theft of gold, there remained a number of loose ends surrounding the murders of Robby's parents.

It was that uncertainty that weighed greatly on the shoulders of Red's best friend.

Chapter 4

The Sugar Lodge

The resort Kate had inherited, The Sugar Lodge, also known as the Sugar Island Resort, had become a landmark on the island. It had started out over forty years earlier as a small fishing resort.

When Alex Garos bought it almost thirty years ago, the whole establishment consisted of a single twelve-unit log cabin. Garos liked it because of the large parcel of real estate on which that log cabin was built—a hundred and forty acres, with twelve hundred feet fronting the St. Mary's River.

As soon as he took possession, Garos razed the log cabin, replacing it with an impressive stone structure many times the size of the original, more rustic building.

And then, as the resort's popularity increased, Garos constructed an even larger building, one that eventually included a five-star restaurant.

Garos didn't stop making improvements. He added a third and a fourth building on the same campus, making the resort one of the finest facilities of its type in the Upper Peninsula of Michigan.

Jack and Kate had made provision for Red. He would stay at the resort for the school year, living with the resort's assistant caretakers—Jim and Mary Fletcher. Jack had hired the Fletchers ostensibly to assist the Lundgrens at the resort, but their primary responsibility was actually to look after Red. Initially, the county did not view the arrangement favorably, but they eventually came around when all other alternatives were deemed futile.

And even though Jack had a condo in Chicago, he spent as much time as he could at the resort.

Ultimately Jack planned to move to Sugar Island—when he totally retired. But his obligations in Chicago were far more than loose ends. He still maintained a very lucrative private security service there. Plus, he owned a half-interest in a downtown Chicago bar.

It was going to take him a little time to make the transition permanent.

But on this day neither Jack nor Kate was thinking about their obligations on the other side of the Sugar Island Ferry—especially Jack. He was cooking.

Neatly assembled on his island-cabinet work area were all the ingredients he would need. These included white wine, extra virgin olive oil, a full pound of butter, several fresh lemons, coarse and fine sea salt, recently purchased peppercorns, and a dozen particularly large carefully filleted whitefish.

He had placed the fish in a clear glass bowl and covered them with three layers of paper towel, which he kept moist by splashing water on it.

He had turned the oven off after he had removed the ten uniformly sized russet baked potatoes. They were perfect. An hour and a half earlier he had scrubbed the potatoes in cold water, pierced each of them four times on each side with a fork, rubbed them with butter, rolled them in coarse sea salt, and placed them uncovered on an open rack of his conventional oven—which was preheated to three hundred and fifty degrees. He then slid a piece of aluminum foil beneath the potatoes to catch any drippings.

Because they were all exactly the same size, he knew that the baking would be approximately sixty minutes.

When his timer went off, he inserted a meat thermometer into the middle potato and verified that it had reached two hundred and ten degrees. The potatoes were done. He then removed them from the oven and placed them in a glass bowl, covered the bowl with foil, and placed it on the range between the burners to maintain heat.

Prior to his having handled the fish, Jack had tossed a fresh salad, sealed it in a covered plastic bowl, and slid it in the refrigerator.

He was looking forward to a quiet Sugar Island night with Kate and the boys.

* * *

Kate, Red, and Red's friend Robby had been out fishing in the St. Mary's River but with only moderate success. At least as far as catching fish was concerned.

But if you were to ask Kate about it, she would tell you the fishing trip was *magnificently* productive—just what she'd had in mind, in fact. Even though they were forced to release all but two of the day's catches. They were just too small.

And as far as the two keepers were concerned—both Kate and Red would have tossed them back as well, had they been theirs to free. Robby had caught the only two fish of any considerable size.

The reason Kate was so pleased with the day had everything to do with giving Robby some time away from his problems. Two uncomplicated hours in a fourteen-foot fishing boat served that purpose perfectly.

Robby was well on his way to recovering from the burns he had suffered as the result of the bomb that had killed his mother. The only physical scars he still bore were on his torso—a couple on his stomach and one large pink wound on his back. And they were healing nicely.

Kate's concern about Robby was focused on the boy's emotional scars resulting from the murders of his parents—and the gnawing realization that the killer or killers still had not been brought to justice. And not only had no arrests been made, but she was quite certain there were no suspects.

Initially, Sheriff Green made it clear to Jack and Kate that he regarded them as little more than an annoyance and that he wished they'd leave Sugar Island. But when it became clear that he was not making any progress on the case, he decided to encourage the Handlers' efforts on his behalf—but not *officially*, of course.

"Mmmm," Kate sighed as they approached the cottage where they stayed. "Do you guys smell that?"

"Sure do, Kate," Robby declared. "Do you think your dad will cook the fish I caught?"

"Maybe, if you clean them," Kate replied. "You do know how to clean fish?"

"Sure," Robby replied. "Dad always made me clean what I caught. But whose car is that in the driveway? I don't recognize it.

"Good question," Kate said. "Must be someone to see Jack."

"Hey, Dad. How long before dinner?" Kate asked as she walked in through the door. Rather than answering her question, he glanced to her left and behind her. Kate followed his eyes.

Initially, she had not seen the two men who were sitting at the kitchen table. One quick glance told Kate a great deal. Both men were wearing gray suits.

No one wore suits on Sugar Island.

Chapter 5
The suits

That strongly suggested they were not residents of Sugar Island. Unless, of course, there had been a funeral that she didn't know about.

One suit was a custom-made wool pinstripe. *Five grand, easy*, she thought. The other was also a nice pinstripe but definitely off the rack. *A thousand at most.*

She guessed they were both from New York because she thought she recognized the custom job as the work of William Fioravanti.

"Oh, I'm sorry. I didn't know we had company."

"Have the boys wash up," Jack requested. "I'm just about finished with dinner. Our guests were about to leave."

The two men exchanged glances at Jack's comment, and then the older one said, "You're Jack's daughter—Kate. Your name is Kate. Right?"

"That's right. And how do you know me?"

"I'm sorry for not introducing you," Jack said. "Kate, this is Harold Festerman. And his assistant, David Nacow. They are attorneys representing Pam Black—Reg's widow."

"Wow, you're a long way from home," she said.

"And so are you. You're a New York City detective, a homicide detective. Right?"

"How is it I know you?" Kate asked.

"Harold is—was—an associate of Reg's, from decades ago," Jack said. "And he's an old friend of mine as well. You probably remember him from our time in Chicago. Harold started practicing law in Chicago back when you were a baby."

"Okay," Kate said. "That makes sense. I'll bet we both looked a little younger back then."

"For sure, I did. I had a full head of hair back then. And I was thirty pounds lighter."

"What sort of law do you practice?"

"Pretty general stuff. I've taken a wide range of cases."

"Mr. Festerman is here to discuss the possible exhumation of Reg's body," Jack said.

"I thought Reg was buried at Calvary Cemetery in Brooklyn."

"Actually Calvary Cemetery is located in Queens, but you're close," Festerman said, correcting her.

"Well, Brooklyn and Queens are both a long way from Sugar Island."

"But your dad is *here*, and Pam wanted me to talk to him personally, to get his opinion on the problem at hand."

"Who wants to dig up poor old Reg, anyway?" Kate inquired.

Chapter 6

The problem

"Mr. Festerman isn't *exactly* sure who is behind it. He just knows that Pam is not eager to give the effort her blessing," Jack said, answering her question. He did not want Festerman to say the wrong thing.

"And why should she?" Kate retorted. After pouring a hot cup of coffee from the freshly made brew on the counter, Kate then joined the two men at the table. She found the topic of conversation intriguing and wanted to hear more.

She took her dark brown hair out of the ponytail, pushed her sunglasses on top of her head, and rolled up the sleeves of her white shirt. Her actions served notice that she intended to become more than a passive bystander.

"It seems to me like an invasion of privacy," she added.

"That's how Pam sees it too," Jack said. "Harold is here to see if we could provide him with some ammunition that might help him block the exhumation."

"I don't know much about that stuff," Kate said. "Do we have any concrete information as to who might be behind it?"

"We don't *know*, but we can guess," Jack said. "We both think that Allison Fulbright is the one pushing for it. At the time he was shot, Reg was under contract to Allison. Apparently Reg received a considerable advance for the job but was shot and killed before it was consummated."

Allison Fulbright was a former first lady—the wife of President Bob Fulbright. The contract to which Jack referred was for the assassination of Barry Butler, the sitting president. Jack was not about to share that information with them.

"So, she wants to get her money back?"

"That's the general idea," Jack said. "After all, the job was not completed. She probably wants to use it to finance her own campaign. Or for who knows what."

"But what good would it do to dig up poor old Reg? It's been a year now since he was shot. What does she have in mind—selling his burial suit?"

"No one really knows how her mind works. But one thing is for sure—Allison does not do anything without a good reason. She must believe that there is some clue buried with Reg. One that might lead to the money she gave him."

"Doesn't she need a court order to have him exhumed?" Kate asked.

"That's right," Festerman replied. "And with her connections, no doubt she could get one, but she wants to keep her name out of it. She is attempting to convince Reg's widow that it would be in her, that is *Pam's*, best interest to request that her husband's body be disinterred. Nacow here informs me that someone has offered to pay Pam fifty thousand dollars to make an official request."

"But it would still have to be deemed warranted. Right?" Kate inquired.

"That wouldn't be a challenge for Allison," Jack said. "All she would have to do is throw a little money at the right judge, and she could facilitate Pam's obtaining the order. Her issue is that she wants the process to remain totally disassociated from her. For her to disclose her interest in Reg's death would attract unwanted attention."

"However," Festerman jumped in, "if she can convince Pam to file the application, then her connection to the matter remains off the radar."

"Can't the widow just refuse the request?" Kate asked.

Chapter 7
Complications

Sure, if she wants to bring down the wrath of the former first lady on her," Jack replied. "Pam literally fears that she might be joining her husband at Calvary Cemetery if she continues to object."

Kate suddenly recalled that while still living in Chicago she had seen her father and this man talking and planning on a few occasions. And Reg would usually be right in the middle.

Reg she had trusted—totally. She knew that her father and Reg were like brothers. Actually closer than most brothers, in some respects. If Reg were sitting at the kitchen table now, instead of this Harold fellow, Kate would have no reservations.

But she was not yet sure she could trust these men.

"What Harold is looking for from us," Jack continued, "are some delay tactics—something that will effectively postpone the excavation until a more permanent fix is found. Pam convinced him that we could help."

Kate thought about it for a moment before responding. She was wondering just how much she should trust this Harold.

"I really think that I need some time to think about this," Kate finally said.

Before she entered that discussion in front of their two visitors, she wanted to discuss the matter more fully with her father.

Besides, she noted that her father had not actually offered any possible solution to the problem. She detected that while he was certainly concerned about Pam's situation, he had not joined the two men at the table—not physically nor conversationally in support.

That suggested to Kate that he also might have reservations regarding one or both of them.

"Are you two going to be in town for a few days?" Jack asked.

"That depends," Harold said.

"On what?"

"We're registered at the hotel for tonight only. I can extend it, if you think I should."

"Why don't you spend tonight there—at the hotel—and then check out in the morning. I'll make arrangements for you to stay here at the resort until we've come to some conclusion. What do you think?"

"Sure. If that works for you."

"Kate and I'll rattle this around a bit this evening. You can check in tomorrow. And then join us for dinner tomorrow evening."

"Best offer we've had. Anything else you need from us *before* tomorrow?"

"No. Like I said, Kate and I'll discuss it and see if we can come up with a solution, or at least some suggestions. I'll make the reservation simply under 'Harold'. Maybe we can get some fishing in before you leave. That is if Kate and the boys didn't catch all the fish in the river."

Kate responded to Jack's teasing with a pleasant but affected smile.

"I'd be up for that," Harold replied as he stood to leave. "We didn't bring gear—is that a problem?"

"I'm sure we can fix you up. We'll talk more about it later. Over dinner."

Chapter 8

Meeting over

Festerman correctly surmised that Jack thought the time had come for him to leave, and he had no desire to overstay his welcome. In fact, he wasn't really confident that there had been much of a welcome to begin with.

Jack tolerated Harold and his associate only because of his enduring respect for Reg and his widow. He knew that Pam would be undergoing a great deal of anguish, even suspecting that she was up against two of the most formidable forces in the world—Allison Fulbright and her husband.

Pam fully understood how her late husband feared the Fulbrights. She correctly assumed that to go against the will of the former first lady could mean an untimely demise.

So, while Jack did not feel fully comfortable with his two visitors, he would do what he could to help them in their effort to bail Pam out of her situation. As far as he was concerned, he could not understand why Allison was so adamant about popping the lid off Reg's coffin. But he reasoned that if Allison wanted to dig Reg up, she must have a good reason to do so, and that her reason might not be a righteous one.

"See you tomorrow … sometime. No need to rush. I'll make sure the room is ready for you first thing in the morning. You can check in whenever it is convenient."

"That's great," Harold replied. "And what time should we be here, for dinner that is?"

"Make it seven. And bring your appetite. I'm cooking up my whitefish specialty—again. You'll love it."

"I'm sure we will."

The two men, wasting no time with further small talk, headed out the door.

Harold did not actually dislike his younger associate. But it was clear that they were not friends.

In fact, initially Harold did not even want to take the younger man with him to visit Jack. The problem was that Harold felt obligated to include David Nacow, because that's what Pam wanted.

Because of his long-standing friendship with Reg, Harold regarded Pam's well-being as his personal responsibility. However, because his office was in Chicago, he requested she contact Nacow for any of her day-to-day legal matters. He had met Nacow several years earlier at a conference he had attended in New York. Harold liked the way the young lawyer carried himself, and he referred Pam to him.

So when Pam called Harold to request that he contact Jack in person regarding the exhumation issue, Harold felt it appropriate to include the younger lawyer on this trip.

Besides, Pam liked Nacow. Were Harold not to take him on the trip to consult with Jack, she would wonder why he was slighting the young man.

And Harold was a gentleman. While he never really sought out Nacow's views on matters of importance, he would not cavalierly dismiss them either.

Chapter 9

The trip back

Festerman and Nacow were very pleased with their visit. They reasoned that Jack would not have invited them back the next day if he didn't intend to help them—if not through personal involvement, at least with some good suggestions.

Festerman, in particular, liked what they had accomplished. He knew from past experience that once Jack got on board, things happened.

And he had good reason to think Jack was at least sympathetic to their cause. After all, he had just invited them to move out of their hotel in the Soo and to take a room at Kate's resort on Sugar Island.

Plus, he had asked them to join him and Kate for dinner the

following evening. Jack, they reasoned, would not have done that if he did not intend to help them.

And they were right. Even though Jack felt no sense of obligation to either Festerman or Nacow, he was concerned about their situation because they were representing the interests of Pam Black, whom he truly cared about.

The two men had arranged to meet up at O'Hare early that morning and then take the same flight from ORD to CIU (Chippewa International Airport). After renting an SUV and registering at a local hotel, they gave Jack a call from their hotel and asked if they could come out to Sugar Island and meet with him. Typically Harold would have called in advance of the trip, but this time he decided not to give Jack the option of refusal.

Jack was pleased the meeting was over and that the two lawyers were on their way off the island.

"Are we all set to eat?" Jack asked.

"We are," Kate replied. "For a few minutes I thought you might invite the lawyers to join us tonight."

Jack just smiled.

Chapter 10

The following evening

Have you heard anything from your friends?" Kate asked. "That Harold guy, and … *Madcow?*"

Kate was being facetious. Through the years, Jack had frequently made reference to a Chicago-based shock jock named Matthew Erich "Mancow" Muller. She was not exactly sure how her father came to know "Mancow," but whenever he brought up the name, Kate would counter with something like: "Are you referring to *madcow*? The bovine disease?"

"His name was *Nacow*—David Nacow," Jack countered with a big smile. "And the answer is no. I haven't heard anything from them. Last I knew they haven't checked in either. Maybe you could give the front desk a call and see if they've talked to them. I'm at a critical point here with these fish."

"Wouldn't want you to wreck your reputation," Kate chuckled. "At least when it comes to cooking whitefish. Heaven knows other parts of it could use some help—your reputation, that is. I'll take a walk over and see what I can find out."

Jack had the fillets—four pounds of them—washed and laid neatly in two large baking pans. He took care to be sure they did not touch. He then covered them with paper towels and periodically sprayed them with water to keep them moist.

The oven was preheated to three hundred and fifty degrees.

He crushed seventy-two Ritz crackers (two sleeves) in a bowl and set it aside.

He opened two six-ounce cans of crabmeat and drained the liquid off. Again using paper towels, he dabbed the remaining moisture from the crabmeat.

Earlier he had melted one cup of butter, and then had let it cool a little.

He added the crabmeat to the butter and stirred it in.

Pouring what he knew to be the perfect amounts of salt and pepper into the palm of his hand, he confidently dumped it into the butter-crabmeat mixture and stirred again.

I'm using a different recipe tonight, Jack thought to himself. *At least different from last night's. Variety is a good thing. Wonder if Kate will notice.*

He removed the paper towel from the whitefish and applied

one-quarter of a teaspoon of freshly squeezed lemon juice to each, using the back of a spoon to rub the juice around.

He then prepared to combine the crumbs with the crabmeat mixture, but held off until he could confirm that the guests' arrival was imminent.

Wonder when those fellows will be getting here? he pondered. *Don't want to put the crab-crumbs on the fish until I'm ready to stick them in the oven.*

"Dad," Kate said as she walked back into their unit. "The front desk hasn't heard anything from the guys. And I checked the unit they set up for them. Thought maybe housekeeping let them in. But there was no sign of their arrival."

"Really?" Jack responded, making sure the fish was again covered and moistened. He washed his hands off using a bottle of lemon juice that he had for that purpose. He then washed again using hand soap.

"The desk clerk did have some interesting information," Kate said. "Probably doesn't relate to this situation, but it sure did sound curious to me. … And are you using a different recipe?"

"Handler here," Jack said, answering his cell.

Chapter 11

People have to eat

Jack," the voice on the phone said. "This is Bill Green. Hope I'm not interruptin'."

"You're fine, Sheriff. What can I do for you?"

"We just pulled two suits out of the St. Mary's … east of the locks, just off Sugar Island."

"Really," Jack replied, beginning to spoon out the crabmeat-cracker mixture and spread it onto the whitefish.

Kate could hear the sheriff on her father's cell, and holding up two fingers, she mouthed: "That's what they told me at the front desk—two bodies."

"Why would you be calling me about that?" Jack asked.

"Well, that's a good question—a question for which I don't have a good answer," the sheriff responded. "It just seemed like the right thing to do—call you. Every time someone dies unexpectedly in my county, my first thought is to call Jack Handler. Do you know anything about it?"

"No. Nothing at all. How'd they end up in the river?" Jack asked as he slid the whitefish into the oven.

"Not sure about that," Sheriff Green said. "But they were both shot in the head with a small-caliber bullet … probably a .22. And then they were dumped into the river. At least that's how it looks right now."

Jack set the timer for twenty-five minutes.

"If something comes to mind," the sheriff said, "give me a call."

"I sure will. If I hear anything. Shot with a .22 you say?"

"That's what it looks like—small caliber, but with a lot of velocity. Forensics will know more soon, but for now that's what it looks like. Well, Jack, be sure to call me if you have any ideas about this."

"Sure," Jack said. "Kate and I are just about to have dinner. If something comes to mind I'll call you."

"I'd appreciate it."

"Hey, Sheriff. Who discovered the bodies anyway?" Jack asked, trying to catch the sheriff before he disconnected.

"They were spotted by a freighter headed to Lake Huron. The captain reported it, and the Coast Guard made the pickup."

"I'll be in touch if I hear anything," Jack said, disconnecting.

Jack then removed the cork from a bottle of white wine whose label documented its origin as the Pessac-Léognan district of France, and he poured two glasses.

The timer indicated ten minutes before the fish were done.

"The proverbial shot across the bow?" Kate stated as a question. "Surely they were killed as a warning to us, not because of what *they* knew."

"You're assuming those bodies are our guys?" Jack asked. "Do we know for certain that the sheriff's VICs are Festerman and Nacow? Couldn't they be just a couple unlucky fishermen?"

"You really think that?"

"We'll undoubtedly find out soon enough," Jack replied, setting two plates on the table. "Too bad the boys are at the Fletchers."

"They're having pizza, Dad. I wouldn't worry about them."

Several minutes passed before Kate spoke up: "You're putting me on. You must be convinced that our two no-shows are dead. Or you wouldn't have put the fish in the oven."

"Yeah. I think we should assume that," Jack said. "If not, they're late, and I wasn't going to let those whitefish dry out. Too bad for them."

Neither Jack nor Kate had much to say while they ate.

"I think we agree that Allison had these men killed," Kate finally said.

"That's logical."

"And the reason she had them killed, just how does that relate to us?"

Chapter 12

Some things best left unsaid

Pretty much as you put it. It was a shot over the bow. She wants us to know just how serious she is about digging up Reg's body."

"Would she ever strike out at you?"

Jack took a moment to consider the question and contemplate his answer. "I really doubt it," he said. "I actually think she likes me, in her own way. I think it helps her sleep at night knowing that people like me exist. That if she ever got herself in a bind, a big one, I might be able to fix it for her."

"Then you *have* worked for her in the past?"

"Kitty. There are some things about me that are best left unsaid."

Kate knew when to keep her mouth shut. And this was one of those times. She had no doubt that her father would answer any question she would ask him and that he would do it honestly. He never lied to her or to his friends.

But he had made it clear to her now and at other times that he preferred not to discuss certain things with her—and these included some of the jobs he had taken. She understood that his silence in these areas was as much to shield her as it was to protect himself.

After that exchange, Kate remained silent for several minutes. Her mind carried her back to her first memories of her father. She recalled how difficult it was for her growing up without a mother and how hard her father had worked to keep his little family together.

She remembered her mother only through the stories her father had related to her through the years. It was not until she was in junior high that he explained exactly how Beth, her mother, had died.

She could tell that her father harbored a great deal of guilt because he had not been able to protect the woman he loved. He explained in detail that night in Chicago, when two men attempted to kill him but inadvertently gunned down Kate's mother instead.

As the years passed Kate often pulled out of her closet her shoebox of memories, the contents of which consisted primarily of the pictures she had of her mother. She would not only compare herself to them, but she would make every effort to conform her appearance to the tattered images of her mother.

Finally, she spoke: "About Allison. Let's say that she did have Harold and his friend killed. And that she did it as a warning to us. Sugar Island is a long way from New York City and DC. Yet she was able to reach her tentacles all the way here … to the degree that she was able to contract a pinpoint hit. Does that mean she has contacts here? Or do you think she brought someone in?"

"This was strictly a professional hit. Probably carried out by a crew from the East."

"Crew? You think more than one shooter?"

"Absolutely. With a single hit—the gunman would be working alone. But these guys were hit at the same time. It would take some doing for one man to pull it off, and then to dump the bodies of two grown men. And given the fact that this would be unfamiliar territory for them. I like two working in tandem, or maybe a family. … In fact, I know of just such a crew. It's a father, and his three children—two girls and a boy. And they're based out of the New York area. Very pricey, I've heard."

Kate was thinking. *If Allison was responsible for the murders of Festerman and Nacow, could she also have had something to do with the killings of Robby's mother and father?*

Kate, yielding to the professional homicide detective who resided within her, struggled to dismiss at least temporarily those thoughts as conjecture based on the fact that she could come up with no motive for Allison to be involved in them.

Chapter 13

Allison cannot be responsible for every bad thing

Kate was correct that Sheriff Green had turned up no credible leads regarding the murders of Robby's parents. And even though he suspected that the killings of the boy's parents were probably perpetrated by the same person or persons, the two events occurred in different counties.

The bombing of Robby's mother's car occurred on M-123 between Paradise and the Lower Tahquamenon Falls—that was in Chippewa County, for which Sheriff Green was responsible, while the boy's father was killed in Luce County. The line dividing Luce and Chippewa Counties ran right through the Upper Tahquamenon Falls complex.

Little Lake Harbor, where the boat belonging to Robby's father was scuttled and burned, lies several miles inside Luce County. That meant that Sheriff Green had no jurisdiction over the case. Besides, because the boat was initially hijacked, the FBI almost immediately took over that case. Plus, the FBI has a reputation for never sharing information.

For some reason, the FBI did not tie the Little Lake murders to the bombing, even though the explosion killed the wife of one of the Little Lake victims. Had the car bombing been regarded as an act of terrorism, then it would have been pulled into federal jurisdiction. But that did not happen.

Both the Handlers and the sheriff suspected that the federal agency separated the two investigations because they believed that the two crimes were not perpetrated by the same people. Jack and Kate were not so sure about that.

"Dad," Kate finally said, "is there any chance that Allison is somehow involved with our other case up here—the Little Lake murders, and the bombing of Robby and his mother?"

Jack understood her thought pattern. In investigations such as these it is always prudent to look for connections. Here they had two members of the same family, murdered only a day apart and in the same general geographic area. And then the killing of the two lawyers—to not at least consider the possibility of a connection would be careless.

"This is convoluted," Jack replied. "I'll grant that. But I am pretty certain that your kidnappers were after the gold treasure that Titus Gordon found at the bottom of Lake Superior. And thanks to your efficient use of OPWs, most of that group is dead. And those who aren't dead have most certainly left the area. But I don't think they were in any way connected to the deaths of Robby's parents.

"I also don't think that the murders of Nacow and Festerman are connected to—"

"Hold on a second," Kate interrupted. "*OPWs*—I'm not familiar with that term. What are they?"

Chapter 14

OPWs

Other people's weapons," Jack replied through an obvious smirk.

"Oh, very clever. You just made that up, didn't you?"

"Actually no. It's not a new term, or even a new concept for that matter. Professionals prefer weapons that cannot be traced back to them. In this case, the fact that you never used a personal weapon will save you a lot of inconvenience. Had you used one of your firearms, it would have been confiscated and held as evidence, for who knows how long. That would not have sat well with your boss."

Jack was teasing her about her recent violent encounters in part to gently lead his daughter away from her well-intentioned interest in his security business. She knew that he contracted his services to various people and entities and that he made a lot of money doing it. But that was the extent of her knowledge regarding it.

But Jack's gentle distraction had worked. Kate was ready to cease being reminded about the people she had recently killed.

"I'm prepared to drop that issue whenever you are. I think you'd agree that I did what I had to do. In every case, I was left with no choice. They were all totally justified."

"I'll drop it," Jack replied. "But with regard to your question. I have no doubt that the group we encountered earlier—the people who kidnapped you and Robby—were from out East, and that their sole interest was the gold.

"If they got what they came for, and I think they got the gold that Mr. Gordon had found, then the remaining members of that group are of no further concern to us at this time. If they think that there might be more gold on the bottom of Lake Superior, they might come back for it. But, should they return, they will likely approach it from the Canadian side."

"You think that there is more gold down there?" Kate asked.

"If Gordon was right, that those gold ingots *were* dropped there when an ancient Minoan ship sunk, probably during a November storm, then the odds are good that more than one such ship went down. Those old wooden ships would be highly susceptible to the northern winds of Lake Superior.

"But my point is this," Jack continued. "To answer your question—I think it unlikely that Allison had anything at all to do with the kidnapping. I think that it was connected to a Russian crime family. The Russians and the Chinese are after gold in a big way. Not that Allison isn't. But that business does not look like her work.

"And the other parts of the puzzle?"

Chapter 15

The trick is to compartmentalize

"You know what I'm talking about," Kate continued. "The car bombing and murders on board the *Snoopy*—those also are not related to Allison either. At least not in my opinion.

"*Whoever* is responsible for the murders of Gordon and his wife, and those on board the *Snoopy*, they committed their acts for reasons yet unknown."

"The trick is to compartmentalize," Jack said.

"Compartmentalize. I know what that means," Kate replied. "But how does it relate to this situation?"

"First of all, don't misinterpret what I am suggesting. Allison must be taken very seriously. Those who do not end up like Festerman and his friend.

"But she must be considered in her own context. Her *only* interest is in getting *her* money back. And anyone who interferes with that effort will suffer. But I think we can be *very* certain that the murders of Robby's parents are not in any way the work of her hand—directly or indirectly. They were altogether too messy and unprofessional."

"So, you think we should just drop Allison for now?" Kate asked.

"It's not going to matter what we do at this point. When she's ready, she will call me," Jack said. "Sooner or later. She knows that Pam trusts me. I am quite certain that Allison will eventually try to buy my influence."

"Is it for sale?"

Jack did not appreciate his daughter's idealism, but he understood it.

"Here's the thing. Allison will *make* this exhumation happen. If Pam tries to stand in the way, she will get hurt. … I owe it to Reg to try to help his family. When your vacation's over, I think I'll fly east with you and pay Pam a visit."

"Vacation!" Kate said sarcastically. "This has been some kind of vacation."

Kate's comments were cut short by the tromping of two teenage boys on the back deck.

"Hey! The boys are back in town," she said with a note of joy in her voice. "These guys always cheer me up. And tonight I could use some cheering up."

"Hey, guys," she said, as Red and Robby barged through the door. "Are you hungry?"

"We're good," Robby said. "Mrs. Fletcher cooked spaghetti."

"Spaghetti, huh. I'd figured it'd be pizza." Kate said. "I'll bet you two Huckleberry Finns liked that."

"She gave us a choice—pizza or spaghetti. We chose spaghetti, and it was GREAT!" Robby exclaimed with a huge smile. "She's the best!"

"Yes, she is," Kate agreed. "And what's that you have in your hand? I'll bet it's something you want to show us."

Robby had walked in the door holding a large envelope in front of him, as though attempting to attract Kate's attention with it.

"Red and I found this online," Robby said. "We used Mrs. Fletcher's computer—*with* her permission—and she let us print it out."

"Wonderful," Kate said with a smile. "I'm glad you got her permission, otherwise she won't be cooking any more of that fine spaghetti for you fellows, and that would be a real shame. Let's see what you've got."

Chapter 16
The Newberry Tablet

This is a picture of a thing they call the Newberry Tablet. It was found near Newberry. That's just west of Tahquamenon. In 1890. Some think it dates from 1500 BC, or even before. It was written in an ancient language. Take a look and tell me what you think?"

The mention of the Newberry Tablet got Jack's attention, and he walked over to Kate's side and examined the image over her shoulder.

The two boys were excited about the find—Red was energized mostly because his friend was so visibly animated.

Robby's fingers shook as he set the picture down in the middle of the square-topped oak dining room table so that all four of them could view it at the same time.

"Listen to this," he said as he began to read the caption under the picture:

"The Newberry Tablet was discovered just north of Newberry, Michigan, in November 1896. It was photographed, and the photo was sent to the Smithsonian Institute. Scientists at the Smithsonian stated they were unclear as to what it was. In fact, initially they declared it to be a hoax. Unfortunately, it was left in a barn for years, where it degraded substantially. And now, parts of it are thought to be kept in a museum located in St. Ignace.

"It has since been discovered that it is written in an ancient script known as a Cypriot Minoan Syllabary. To find this ancient syllabary in Michigan when it disappeared from the Mediterranean in about 500 BC is just like finding a fingerprint of the Minoan Traders."

Both Jack and Kate were well aware of the Smithsonian and what it represented. Established in 1846 "for the increase and diffusion of knowledge," the Smithsonian consists of a group of numerous museums, research institutions, zoos, and hundreds of affiliated facilities throughout the world.

The website Robby was reading from was created by a man named Roger Jewell, one of the most outspoken proponents for the theory that Minoan traders transported to Europe great quantities of Lake Superior copper.

Mr. Jewell, while not an academic, did receive his BS degree in forestry management from the University of Minnesota and subsequently worked for thirty-two years for the US Forest Service. Many of those years he spent in Michigan's Upper Peninsula.

He served for twelve years as the district ranger for the Sault Ste. Marie District of the Hiawatha National Forest. The Hiawatha National Forest is huge, encompassing parts of seven counties and covering over 894,000 acres.

During his tenure in Michigan, Jewell grew fascinated with numerous stone formations and artifacts that suggested to him that an early European civilization influenced that region. That notion, coupled with the fact that there is evidence indicating that millions of pounds of copper had been mined thousands of years before Christopher Columbus, and that copper bearing the DNA of Michigan's Upper Peninsula has turned up throughout Europe dating from the pre classical Greek period, led Jewell to do some research.

He determined that the culture was Minoan, and that it probably took place as a result of the international desire for copper.

Best-selling author Gavin Menzies has announced that his next book will provide further evidence that the Minoans were heavily engaged in copper mining and trading as early as 2200 BC and that the mines were largely centered in the Lake Superior area.

So, Robby was eager to demonstrate that his father was not alone in his theory regarding Minoan copper activity, and that the shipwreck he discovered might have been the real thing.

Robby then took a step back, looked first at Kate, and then looked at Jack. "What do you think, Mr. Handler? Could my father have been right?"

Jack was a self-professed skeptic—he was never quick to buy into new theories, particularly those heralded on the Internet.

And Kate was a lot like him in that respect. When confronted by a friend or associate with a novel idea, which she suspected had been introduced over some obscure blog, she was frequently known to retort, "Well, you know what Abraham Lincoln said—you can believe only half of what you read online."

Nevertheless, both Jack and Kate were savvy enough to realize that many important scientific discoveries were actually made by non-scientists, and that frequently those charged with the job of keeping the gate for the various scientific disciplines were both jaded and lazy—characteristics that often led them to put turf protection ahead of objectivity.

So, they withheld judgment. While Kate poured two hot cups of freshly brewed coffee and grabbed two glasses of lemonade for the boys, Jack pulled out the chairs around the table. Both he and Kate had determined they'd listen to the boys and keep open minds.

"Mr. Handler," Robby said. "Red and I were thinking. I've got a lot of hiking gear at my house. When do you think I could go get it?"

Jack was impressed that Robby did not ask "if" he could pick up his equipment; rather he assumed that he could and went directly to the "when."

Flashing a smile and wink at Kate, he asked, "What *exactly* do you fellows have in mind?"

Chapter 17
What could this be?

The boys wanted to do some exploring, but they were afraid to share their precise thoughts with Jack and Kate for fear of getting their plan shot down.

Besides the evidence regarding Minoan copper mining along Lake Superior, they had read that there were numerous other sorts of Minoan artifacts sprinkled throughout the Upper Peninsula.

For instance, dozens of Bronze Age spears and arrowheads had been found from Michigan to the Atlantic Ocean. These Bronze Age finds suggested, according to Robby's father, that Minoan copper mining did take place during this period—approximately 2500 to 1500 BC.

And the fact that such finds were limited to the area east of the supposed copper mines further supported his theory that the shipping route used to transport the copper back to Europe was along the St. Lawrence Seaway.

The boys thought that if they could find even one bronze tool or weapon in the vicinity of the supposed copper mines, it might help vindicate the work of Robby's deceased father.

Chapter 18

The challenge

Ever since he discovered the ancient shipwreck near that of the Edmund Fitzgerald, Titus Gordon was determined to demonstrate the validity of his find and veracity of his theory.

Perhaps if establishment scholarship had been even a little bit open to the possible legitimacy of the wreck that he had found, then he might have been willing to accept their conclusion that the shipwreck was not that of a Bronze Age shipping vessel.

But when he first attempted to publish his findings in a scholarly journal, the editor rejected his paper, insisting that he have the shipwreck itself authenticated by a reputable authority.

That's when he first contacted Dr. Henry.

Initially, the professor refused even to look at the pictures, stating that it was totally impossible that the supposed shipwreck was that of a Minoan vessel. "Minoan merchants could not possibly have navigated their way from the Atlantic Ocean into Lake Superior," Dr. Henry argued. "It was simply an impossibility. The shipwreck images had to have been forged."

Public pressure was so great, however, that Dr. Henry finally agreed to meet with Gordon and to examine the images.

Gordon naïvely assumed that his pictures would be given a fair hearing. But that did not happen.

The very moment he handed the images he had taken of the shipwreck to Dr. Wilbur Henry, the professor barely even looked at them before casually dismissing them as frauds.

Not only did Dr. Henry inform Gordon to his face, but before the end of the day he called a press conference and formally announced that the much-heralded find was nothing more than a hoax and that Titus Gordon was responsible for creating it.

Gordon was humiliated. He had waited his entire life for something like this to come his way. He had posted his pictures on several blogs, and without exception every comment posted was positive.

Dr. Henry had made preparations for the press conference well before he met with Gordon and had even prepared his initial comments before having seen the images.

Gordon felt ambushed. Initially, he tried to enlist the help of a different expert. But no other scholar with credentials in the field would even talk to him. He was left with Dr. Henry. Other scholars informed him that if his find were ever to be documented, he would have to go through Dr. Henry to accomplish it.

So, it was back to the blogs for Titus Gordon.

Weeks passed, and he received thousands of posts from all over the world. But no recognized authority offered to help.

Finally, Gordon went directly to Dr. Henry's students. One after another of the professor's students became convinced of the legitimacy of the images Gordon had taken of the supposed Minoan shipwreck. They exerted sufficient pressure on the professor that it was making life difficult for him in the classroom.

At last he agreed that if Gordon would make arrangements to send the mini-sub down a second time, he would take part in the endeavor and then render an opinion based on firsthand knowledge.

Gordon agreed to the terms. Unfortunately for him, in order to finance the dive, he was forced to sell one of the ingots of gold that he had brought up from the shipwreck. Up to that point, he had not even revealed that he had removed gold from the wreckage.

Had he been willing to have fortune without fame, he could have used his find to finance a wealthy lifestyle for himself and his heirs. But he wanted the credit for his find as well.

He thought that if he melted down the ingot and recast it into smaller ingots, he could destroy all the markings on the gold and dispose of it piecemeal.

But gold has its own identifying characteristics. And once people with the proper instruments got their hands on it, they could determine with reasonable accuracy its date and place of origin.

Chapter 19

Black sand

In this case, it appeared to be beach placer gold, taken from North America. Beach placers (pronounced "plas-ers") are formed in sand and gravel deposited along the edge of large bodies of water, generally in "black sand."

Most likely the body of water from which this gold was removed would have been Lake Superior.

The date of removal was less certain. But the fact that it was taken from a beach placer suggests that it was a primitive people who harvested it, as opposed to its having been removed by modern mining methods.

And because it had been recently recast, and because it was not in the form of coins, the people doing the testing were compelled to believe that there might be a lot more of it.

And they were right. Gordon had produced for sale nearly five pounds of gold. He reasoned that would pay the cost of equipment rental for the dive, plus easily take care of his living expenses for the next year. Even without that five pounds, Gordon still had nearly two thousand pounds (or about forty million dollars' worth) hidden at his house.

Once Ivan, the Russian gold oligarch, found out about it, he immediately dispatched a crew to the Upper Peninsula to find and capture all of Gordon's gold.

Even though the Russians did successfully loot the treasure, the final chapter had not yet been written on Gordon's legacy.

Robby and Red knew they would never get the gold back. Besides, they weren't interested in the money. They wanted (or more specifically, *Robby* wanted) to restore Titus Gordon's place in history as the man who established as fact the existence of the Minoan copper-shipping network between Michigan's Upper Peninsula and throughout the Atlantic and Mediterranean regions.

All they had to do to accomplish that was to engage their innate ichneutic skills to find a substantial cache of Minoan bronze artifacts near the Lake Superior copper mines.

Under any normal conditions that might seem an insurmountable task for two fourteen-year-old boys—but not for Robby and Red. They had a plan. And they had resolve.

"I think they've still got your house secured as evidence," Jack said. "What do you propose we do? Go there in the dead of night, and break in?"

Chapter 20

The plan

"Actually," Kate countered as she got up from the table and topped off the coffees with the last of the pot, "the Gordon residence is not *actually* a crime scene. And it is in Sheriff Green's jurisdiction. He's such a fan of yours, Dad, I'll bet that if we took the boys and met him over there, he'd be happy to let Robby pick up some of his personal belongings. God knows he's going to need some of his clothes for school this fall."

"I don't know about his being a 'fan,'" Jack chuckled. "But I wouldn't be at all surprised if he would do that. I'll give him a call in the morning and check with him."

Robby and Red exchanged a quick, nervous glance.

"Okay, boys," Jack said. "I want you to tell me what this is all about. You've got more in mind than picking up some camping equipment. Spill it."

Red knew better than to try to mislead his uncle and Kate, so he looked at his friend with eyebrows raised and mouth squeezing out an affected smile—the sign that Robby should explain to Jack and Kate the nature of their plan.

"Mr. Handler," Robby said. "I would like to pick up my camping gear. Dad and I used to go camping a lot, in the national forest—Hiawatha. And I think Red and I could use it yet this summer … (slowly dropping his voice) to ummm, do some camping."

"But that's not all, is it?" Jack asked.

"Well, we have three trail bikes—Dad's, Mom's, and mine. I thought we could pick up two of them. I could ride Dad's. And Red could ride mine. I think we could have a lot of fun with them."

"I see," Jack said. "But there's *still* more. Right?"

Red was nodding his head.

"We would like to take Dad's metal detector into the Hiawatha National Forest—the *western* section. Dad and I used to go to the *eastern* section a lot. But my grandfather took my dad to the western part—that's where they spent a lot of time."

"Camping out?" Kate asked.

"Yes, and exploring."

"Exploring what?" Kate asked.

"He told me about a stone formation out there. It's just off the North Hiawatha Trail, about two miles north of M-94. He and my grandpa found it when he was digging to build a fire. Thirty years ago. Back when you could build fires in the park.

"Once, when I was probably four or five, he and Grandpa took me with them. I don't remember much about it—nothing about it was special, at that time. But I did go there.

"He said that the first time he found it, it just looked like some flat stones had been laid on the ground. But when he started digging it up, he discovered it was huge. They spent two days with shovels, and he said that it looked a lot like one of those solstice stone chambers, like they've found out East. They had to get back, so they just shoveled all the dirt back."

"You think you could find it again?" Kate asked.

"Not from memory. But I have a map," Robby replied. "It's in my hiking equipment. Red and I were just thinking that maybe we could spend a day or two exploring. I think we could find it. And if I take a metal detector, maybe we can find some bronze or copper artifacts. If we did find something, it could help prove my dad's theory. Because, according to what I've read, bronze was not part of the Native American heritage—not for tools or for weapons."

There was silence for a brief moment around the table. The boys had their fingers crossed for luck, figuring this was a long shot—getting permission to spend a few days and nights in the woods on their own. Red was experienced in the outdoor life, having to fend for himself after his parents were killed in a house fire. But Robby was much less knowledgeable about survival in the wild.

Jack finally spoke up. "Sounds like a ton of fun to me—I'll call the sheriff in the morning." Then, looking down to check his watch, he had another thought. "I've got his cell, I'll ask him now."

Chapter 21

Good memories

The only time the sheriff could make it was early the following morning. Jack asked Kate whether she wanted to go with them to the Gordon house or perhaps stay home to avoid further conflict with the sheriff.

"You've gotta be kidding," she said. "I wouldn't miss this opportunity."

That's how Jack viewed it as well—as an opportunity to gain further insights into the way the Gordon house functioned. And, quite possibly, find a clue.

The drive from Sugar Island to Robby's house was about fifty miles. Given that the sheriff wanted them to be there at exactly seven-thirty a.m. meant that they would need to leave the resort by six, because there was no way to gauge with any degree of certainty just how long it might take for the ferry to dock and for them to get off.

So Jack informed the boys that he'd be waking them up at five-thirty. The two boys looked at each other and nodded their agreement.

The next morning, when Jack entered the kitchen to grind his ritual coffee, he was shocked to find Robby and Red already sitting at the table with empty cereal bowls between their elbows. It was barely five-thirty, and both were set to go.

Kate walked in right behind him, equally surprised to find the boys up and ready to go.

"Holy smoke," Jack said, feigning shock. "You two go to bed last night, or did you just stay up eating?"

"We went to bed," Robby answered. "But I didn't sleep very well."

"I can understand that," Jack said. "It's been a while since you've been back to your house. How do you think you'll hold up?"

"Fine. I'll be fine. I'm eager to go back and get some of my stuff. Just how much do you think the sheriff will let me take?"

"As much as you can until he stops you," Jack replied. "If you confine yourself to your room, he probably won't stop you right away. … Where do you store your camping gear—in the garage?"

"Yeah."

"Let's grab that stuff first," Jack said. "After we get it loaded, I'll coax the sheriff into helping me load the trail bikes into the trailer."

"You won't need help, Mr. Handler," Robby said. "The bikes are very light mountain bikes."

"Oh, that kind of trail bike," Jack replied. "I was thinking Honda two-cycle trail bikes. I'm sure the sheriff won't have a problem with your taking your bicycle.

"The first thing we do," Jack continued while grinding his morning Dancing Crane African Dark. "The first thing is to locate and load the camping equipment. And then the bikes. How many bikes do you have in the garage?"

"A lot of them. Dad never got rid of anything. My rusty fourteen-inch Huffy is still there—training wheels and all."

"We won't want to be indecisive when we get there," Jack continued to instruct. "We want to take *only* two bikes. You come with me and point them out—the bikes and the camping gear. Red and I'll start loading that stuff. And then I'll ask you if you need to pick up some clothes from your room. At that point, Kate, you jump in and say that you will go with him and help him get what he needs for school. And then the three of you go to Robby's room and pack up some of his belongings. I'll stay with the sheriff and see how he's coming on the case."

"Sounds like a plan," Kate replied. "That'll give me a chance to snoop around a little."

"Of course, it's going to depend on the sheriff's mood," Jack concluded.

Jack never liked to leave anything to chance. It was not that he was a control freak. But when there were certain things he wanted to accomplish, he would develop what he considered the most conducive scenario to get done what he wanted to get done.

And in this case, he constructed a plan that he felt would best get them in and out with the desired results. If all went well, and if the sheriff was agreeable, they could sweep in, pick up what they wanted, and get out before the sheriff had the opportunity to protest.

“What exactly will you be looking for in your bedroom?” Jack asked.

“My hiking boots,” Robby said. “And my riding shoes. Dad always insisted on using the proper shoes with strenuous activities. I have shoes I used only when riding and hiking with him. Mom didn’t want me to take my good shoes to camp in case I might lose them.”

Chapter 22
Robby's house

The map. It's in my room—tucked into the toe of one of my riding shoes," Robby replied.

Jack was satisfied with their preparation. He warmed up his coffee and transferred it to his favorite insulated travel mug. Kate had given it to him for Christmas two years earlier.

* * *

The ferry ride was uneventful. The only thing that stood out was the level of silence that engulfed the vehicle as Jack, Kate, and the two boys headed south on I-75 toward M-28.

Robby's home was right on Whitefish Bay, just north of the river mouth where the golden-brown waters of the Tahquamenon River emptied.

Even as a small child Robby enjoyed paddling a canoe up the river, sometimes nearly a mile, and then riding the current back toward his house. That always made his mother nervous. Whenever she saw him dragging the boat toward the water, she would remind him that her father called the lower part of the Tahquamenon the "River of the Head Winds," because, whether you were going upstream or downstream, you always seemed to be bucking a headwind. That was especially troublesome if your boat was a canoe.

Robby's father and mother had inherited the home from her parents. Robby loved living there, but only because it had its own pier. While it was not large enough to tie up boats as large as the *Snoopy*, it was plenty adequate for the eighteen-foot outboard that Titus and Robby used for Saturday morning fishing trips.

The waters of the bay were much calmer than those of Lake Superior. On almost any given morning from late April through late October the bay would be perfectly safe to venture upon. And they did just that—Robby and his father. They fished often.

All of those memories and many more like them raced through Robby's mind as they turned north on M-123. Still, he had not mouthed a single word after the ferry ride. He was thinking of happier times.

Even as they passed over the bridge by Tahquamenon Bay, Robby remained silent. Just before they reached his house, he told Jack that he should start slowing down because his driveway was just ahead.

Jack knew where the house was, but he was relieved to hear Robby engage with the rest of them.

The sheriff was already there. Jack wasn't late, but the sheriff still beat him. He was sitting in his car.

"Thanks for meeting us," Jack said as he walked toward the marked car.

Sheriff Green had already removed the crime scene tape from

the driveway and the front entry and was standing in the driveway beside his car. "Five minutes," he said. "You've got five minutes. And I don't want any of you to get out of my sight. Am I clear?"

"Sounds right, Sheriff," Jack replied. "Shall we start in the garage? We're looking for some camping equipment and a couple bicycles."

The sheriff stopped just before he reached the front door. "Okay, then. We should turn around and head toward the garage."

The garage was detached from the house and was still secured with the yellow tape.

"I'm guessing the bikes would be in the garage then. Right, kid?"

"Yes, sir," Robby responded.

"Okay, Robby," the sheriff said after he had opened the overhead. "See what you're looking for?"

"Right there," Robby said, walking over to where three bikes were fastened to the garage wall. "That's them."

"You can take one," the sheriff said. "Which one's yours?"

"The middle one's mine, but I'd like to take my dad's bike too, so Red and I can go riding. Is that okay?"

"Let me take a closer look at those bikes," the sheriff said, walking up and checking the manufacturer's label. "We had bikes just like these turn up in a burglary case, not long ago."

"These bikes are not stolen," Jack said. "Robby's father bought these legitimately."

"Not what I'm suggesting," the sheriff said. "What I'm getting at is that these are *very* expensive pieces of equipment—five grand each."

Tapping his finger on the cobalt blue frame of one of them, he continued, "Hear that? That's carbon fiber."

And then he spun the front wheel. "Those are *very* grippy tires. And thru-axle forks—those are serious, *very* serious bikes. I'm surprised someone hasn't broken in here and removed 'em. Load all three of them up. I don't want them left here. At least if Jack's got 'em, I'll know where they are if I need them."

Jack and the boys immediately removed the bikes from the unlocked hangers and placed them in Jack's trailer.

"Do you see your camping equipment?" Jack asked Robby.

"Right there," Robby said, pointing to four boxes that were lying on a freshly installed shelf. The gear included two sleeping bags, camping stove, two lightweight backpacks—fully loaded, and a Garrett Infinium Land & Sea Metal Detector with submersible headphones.

"Have these boxes even been opened?" the sheriff asked. "All this stuff looks brand new. When did your dad buy it—the camping equipment, and the bikes?"

"A few months ago," Robby replied. "Dad took Mom and me to Chicago. The bikes were all custom made."

We're looking at close to twenty grand here, Jack calculated. *That's a lot of money to be spending. Must be he did cash in on some of that gold. That's probably what alerted the gold thieves.*

"Sheriff," Kate interjected. "I really would like to pick up some of Robby's clothes. All we've had for the past month is what he had taken to camp. Do you think it'd be okay to grab enough clothes to avoid the department store? I'm afraid he'll run away if I try to take him shopping."

"Sure," the sheriff replied. "Take what you need, but confine it to his room. Don't touch anything outside the kid's room. No snooping around. You and Robby go ahead. Red can stay down here with us. I'll unlock the door.

"Your father and I are going to talk out here about some other business."

This was what Jack was hoping to do—take a little time to see where the sheriff was at in his investigations.

"Red," Jack said. "Why don't you use the straps in the trailer and secure those bikes so they don't bounce around. The sheriff and I are going to talk for a few minutes."

The sheriff then turned and walked toward his brand new black patrol car.

"Jack, you and I need to talk about a few things. Why don't you join me over here."

The two men leaned against the front of the sheriff's car, which was facing the house.

Jack remained silent, giving the sheriff a chance to take the conversation wherever he wished.

Neither man spoke for nearly a minute. Finally, the sheriff began to speak: "I suppose you heard about that cat fight on the ferry a few days ago? What did you make of it?"

Chapter 23

Heart to heart

Quite the scene, I heard," Jack said. "I talked to Bill—the crewman on the ferry. He'd never seen anything like it before. He was sure he was going to have to call you in, but the women stopped fighting as quickly as they had started. Bang—and it was over."

"That's what I heard as well," the sheriff said. "To me, that whole thing didn't sound right. No one had ever seen those women before. All we know about them is that they came onto the island a few hours earlier and then hung out at the Hilltop Bar much of the afternoon. As near as we can tell they didn't drink. They ordered a couple beers, but ended up drinking iced tea. So they weren't drunk."

"Were they by themselves?" Jack asked.

"They were. A couple of the regulars joined them for some

pool. But the young women came in alone."

"Was there anything unusual about the way they left?" Jack asked. "Did they leave alone? You said they stayed there a couple hours. That's a long time to hang out at a bar without drinking. Something must have prompted them to leave."

"I asked the bartender about that," the sheriff said. "She told me that the older one got a call, right in the middle of a pool game. And just like that, the two girls paid their bill, dropped a nice tip, and left."

"I'm sure it was a sight," Jack said. "But why all the interest in two girls fighting? I'm sure that happens every day in a city the size of the Soo."

"Sure it does," the sheriff replied. "But we can usually get to the bottom of these things. It's always the same actors. But *this* time we have two totally unknown good-looking females, a blonde and a redhead, getting into it on the ferry. That's not just unusual—it's unique."

"Sheriff," Jack interrupted. "There's something you're not telling me."

"Well, maybe," the sheriff confessed. "I don't know if it's pure coincidence or not, but we found a car ditched in the woods not far from Barbeau, off South Scenic Drive. In that car we found a receipt that was punched at just about the same time as that girl fight."

"Ditched?" Jack asked. "What do you mean by ditched? Was it abandoned? Broke down?"

"Later model car," the sheriff said. "Good working order. But it was just left there in the woods with the key in the ignition. It was a rental."

“That is strange,” Jack said.

“More than strange. There’s much more to it,” the sheriff said, turning to face Jack. “We found blood in the car. A *lot* of blood. And a bullet hole.”

This caught Jack’s attention.

“When *exactly* did this happen—the fight on the ferry?”

“Just before seven p.m. last Tuesday.”

Jack started thinking. The two lawyers Pam Black had dispatched to talk to him left the resort only thirty minutes prior to the incident on the ferry. And if the abandoned bloody car was on the ferry at the same time, that would not only confirm what he and Kate already suspected regarding the fate of Festerman and Nacow, but it would strongly suggest that the killers actually spent time on Sugar Island.

Jack did not appreciate *that* fact. It was one thing to kill two of his associates, but quite another to do it in his backyard. That, in Jack’s eyes, amounted to more than merely a shot across the bow—it was meant as a stern warning to him and Kate.

“I’m thinking you still have not told me the whole story,” Jack said.

“There is more,” Sheriff Green continued. “You know those bodies I told you about? The ones spotted by the freighter, floating in the St. Mary’s? Well, one of those bodies had got caught up on some trees near the western bank of the channel, near the southern tip of Sugar Island, quite close to Neebish Island. That’s not far from where we found that car.

“The Coast Guard pulled the second one out a little further downstream.”

“Have you identified the bodies?” Jack asked, with the virtual certainty setting in that the bodies were those of Festerman and Nacow, just as they had suspected.

"Yes, I have names," the sheriff said, taking a small piece of paper from his shirt pocket.

"This is what we've got," he continued. "One of the victims was named Harold Festerman. He appears to have been a lawyer with an office in your hometown—Chicago. And the other one, he also was a lawyer. He's from New York—your daughter's neck of the woods."

"I know those men," Jack said.

"I suspected as much," the sheriff said. "Because we found in that abandoned SUV, which, by the way, had been rented by Mr. Festerman, a handwritten note with your name, address, and phone number. Would you mind telling me how that happened? Why they would have your name? Did you have business with these fellows?"

For a moment Jack hesitated. The sheriff might already know more than he was letting on. *Maybe he's fishing. Maybe that's why he was so willing to meet us out here this morning.*

Jack carefully considered what he should share with the sheriff. While Festerman and Nacow were not his clients, which meant that he was not ethically or legally bound by any confidences with regard to the two dead men, still Jack felt constrained to keep Reg's widow and Allison out of the conversation. He realized that he had to be very careful about what he said next.

After what seemed an extended period of silence to both Jack and the sheriff, Jack said, "Festerman and I go back years … to Chicago—twenty-five, thirty years ago. Nacow, I had never met him before. Not before what now appears to have been the day they were murdered.

"The two men had been out to the resort, and I did meet briefly with them. It would appear as though they were headed back to their hotel at the time they were killed."

"What sort of business did you discuss?" the sheriff asked.

"The only *business* we discussed was fishing—I had invited them back out to go fishing the next day. This wasn't exactly a business trip."

Jack then had an idea.

Chapter 24

Jack thinks fast

The younger man," Jack said, "Mr. Nacow, he was from New York, and he was having a difficult time establishing a client base in the city. The two of them had some sort of a relationship. I'm not sure what it was, but Harold viewed Nacow as his protégé.

"Harold knew that I had clients in New York, and he wanted to introduce his friend to me, thinking that I might be able to hook him up with some work—help him make some contacts."

Jack then chuckled. "For some reason Festerman thought that I might know some people in New York who could use a good lawyer."

"Then you did not engage in any specific discussion with either of these two gentlemen?" the sheriff asked.

"Not at that point," Jack answered. "Things might have changed after a few hours in a boat with the young man, but I was not yet ready to recommend him, even with Harold's endorsement. You can tell a lot about a man by watching him fish."

"What was the basis of your initial conversation with Mr. Festerman, before you agreed to meet with him?"

"Harold really didn't say what he wanted to talk about. Good lawyers don't discuss business on the phone. … When he asked to meet with me and to introduce a friend, that was enough."

As he was answering the sheriff's questions, a troubling thought occurred to Jack: *the sheriff is going to have this same conversation with Kate. How is she going to react?*

He would have to give her a heads up.

Chapter 25
The Map

Jeans, shirts, socks, and underwear," Kate said. "Make sure you get the basics."

"It's gone," Robby said, loudly and visibly upset.

"What's gone?"

"The map. Dad had made me a map showing how to find that stone formation in the national forest. I had tucked it into one of my riding shoes—it's not here."

"Are you sure?" Kate asked. "Maybe you put it in one of your other shoes."

"No, that's not possible. I pushed it down in the toe as far as it would go, in my riding shoe. I never rode the trail bike unless I was wearing these shoes—Dad wouldn't let me. He said these shoes would give me proper support for my instep. That was very important to him. These were very expensive. So, Dad told me *specifically* to hide the map in my riding shoe. It was almost like he was expecting something bad to happen to him and he wanted me to be sure to take care of that map. It was in my shoe, and now it's gone."

"That's strange," Kate said, "anything else look out of place?"

"Yes. Everything's moved around, but just a little," Robby said. "I think it's all here, except for the map. But stuff isn't *exactly* where I put it before camp."

"Could your mom have cleaned your room while you were gone?" Kate asked.

"I don't think so. She almost *never* came in my room. We sort of had a deal—I kept it straightened up, and she left my stuff alone."

Kate's detective eyes scoured the room, logging every inch: the single bed covered with an oversized red and green plaid woolen blanket, and an oak dresser, most likely handed down from family members or purchased from an estate sale, the top of which was cleaned off except for a slingshot, an oil lamp, and three books—*Tom Sawyer*, *Old Yeller*, and a guide to hiking trails in the Upper Peninsula.

The room was painted forest green. Kate considered that a perfect color for a teenage boy. Tied-back red and green hand-made curtains provided a nice view of the Tahquamenon River, particularly in the evening.

Robby had several maps taped on his walls. A large silver fox pelt hung above his bed.

On the south wall stood a ceiling-height bookcase filled with sets of Five Little Peppers, Boxcar Children, Sherlock Holmes, and Mark Twain books.

Looks like Robby is quite the reader, Kate concluded. *Never would have guessed that.*

Over his doorway, Robby had mounted a huge rack from a twelve-point buck. It was so large that it hung too low for him to latch his door.

Kate viewed that as highly significant, in that it suggested Robby was so secure in his home that he did not sense the need to shut his door.

Noticing that his closet door was slightly ajar, Kate opened it fully. There, she was amazed to find all of his shirts and jackets hanging neatly, with his boots and shoes tucked underneath.

Above was a well-organized overhead shelf with a dozen or more board games on one end and neatly stacked hats, scarves, and gloves on the other.

Kate then walked over to the window. Robby's bedroom was on the second floor, and his window overlooked the front drive. *Looks like Dad and the sheriff are really getting into it. Wonder what that could be about?*

Turning back to check out what Robby had placed on the bed, and perhaps to speed up his efforts, Kate said, "Well, let's see what you've got here. I think that should about do it. I think you're going to have to pass on the map. Maybe you have a pair of good school shoes?"

"I wear hiking boots to school," Robby said. "I do have another pair of them, but they're pretty small."

"This will be fine," Kate said, stuffing everything into a couple pillowcases. "We should get down there before the sheriff comes up after us."

After ramming the last of his clothes snuggly into the second pillowcase, Robby said, "One more thing—and *this* will come in handy."

"What's that?" Kate asked.

Chapter 26

GPS

My GPS," Robby replied. "Dad put a geocache near the stone formation, to help us find it in case I somehow lost the map."

"Really? How can that help?" she asked, carefully examining Robby's Garmin Montana 650T.

"The same day Dad hid the geocache at the location," Robby explained, "he also hid a little device that sends out a beeping signal that I can pick up when I get close. All I have to do is get within a short distance of it, and it will sort of lead me to it."

"That's what I heard, about geocaching," Kate said. "It's like treasure hunting with a Geiger counter."

"Not exactly," Robby chuckled. "You and Jack should go out geocaching with me sometime. I think you'd have fun. A lot of people are doing it. The geocache even records when people find it, so you can retrieve the information to see who was successful. Usually, the person who hides the geocache provides an encrypted message giving a hint. Sometimes they even provide coordinates. Dad didn't do anything like that. He just wanted me to be able to find the site. That's why he made the map."

"Well, go ahead and stick that in your bag," Kate said. "Chances are the sheriff won't even bother to see what you've got. It appears he is more interested in dealing with my dad right now."

Kate and Robby each tossed a pillowcase over their shoulders and headed downstairs.

As they walked up to where Jack and the sheriff were standing, Jack looked at Kate and intentionally dropped his coffee cup onto the asphalt driveway. It shattered.

Kate knew immediately that her father had given her a signal—she needed to be on guard.

"I can't believe I did that," Jack said. "I hope nothing splashed on you, Sheriff."

"I'm fine," the sheriff said. "I need to have a little talk with Kate now, if you don't mind."

"Not at all. I'll get a broom out of the garage and sweep up the pieces," Jack said, shooting a look of warning at Kate. "Sorry about this mess."

"Kate," the sheriff said, turning his attention to her. "Can I assume that all you have in those bags is the boy's clothing?"

"That's about it, Sheriff," she said. "Robby grabbed a toy or two, but that's it."

"I need to do my duty here," he said. "Why don't you dump it out in the backseat of your vehicle and let me take a quick look. Just doin' my job."

"No problem," Kate said, dumping the contents out of the pillowcase she had carried, while at the same time Robby dumped his.

The sheriff took only a moment to satisfy himself that there was nothing objectionable being removed from the house. He momentarily picked up and examined the Garmin but tossed it back with the clothes.

"That all looks fine," he said. "Son, why don't you stuff your belongings back in the bags while I have a little talk with Kate. Okay?"

Chapter 27

Kate Questioned

Your father and I have been discussing those two men who visited you at the resort Tuesday," he said. "Do you know who I'm talking about?"

"I think so," she said. "There were two men that Dad was talking to. One was an old friend from Chicago. And the other one was a lawyer from New York. Actually they were both lawyers. But the older one, the one from Chicago, he's the only one I'd met before."

"Then you did know at least one of the men?"

"Vaguely. He and my dad were associates years ago, when I

was still living at home."

"Do you know what they were discussing with your father?"

Kate didn't have to pause—she already knew what Jack would want her to say.

"They were going to go fishing—that's about all I know. My dad loves to fish."

"Did they discuss business, or anything else not related to fishing?"

"I came in just as they were preparing to leave. All I know for sure is Dad suggested that they come back the next day, that he would cook up his whitefish specialty, and that they could go fishing the following day. I reserved them a room at the resort, so they could get an early start."

"So, they were staying at the resort?"

"No," Kate said. "Not yet. Dad had suggested that they check out of their hotel the following morning. He asked me to set them up at the Sugar Lodge for the next day. That's about it. You should ask Dad about it; he might remember more than I do."

Kate knew that fishing was always her father's fallback response to almost any question about which he wanted to be vague. Even in Chicago, when Jack sought to provide as little information as possible concerning almost any matter, he would say he was going to take someone fishing.

And he did. He always had his fishing gear ready and his license up to date. Most of Jack's meetings during the warm months were conducted on Navy Pier.

Surprisingly, the fishing was very good off the pier. While in most cities located on large bodies of water, the major rivers pass through the populated areas before dumping into the lake or ocean, that is not the case with the Chicago River. It runs *out* of Lake Michigan and into the tributaries that eventually become the Mississippi River.

So the fish caught off Navy Pier are virtually pollution free.

"Well," the sheriff said, "that's just about what your father said. Is there anything else that you can recall that might be significant, with regard to those two men?"

"No," Kate said. "But maybe if you told me what this was all about. Maybe that would help."

"I'll let your father fill you in on the details," the sheriff said. "I think we're about done here."

"Jack," the sheriff said, walking toward his car. "I might want to talk to you again as this matter unfolds. Don't leave town."

"I'll be around," Jack replied. "But I'm sure I'm not going to have any helpful information about this business. Like I said, I *did* know Harold Festerman, but before this week, the last time I talked to him was at least ten years ago. I have no reason to think that I had anything to do with what got him … *them* killed."

"I'm sure you don't think you had anything to do with their deaths, Handler," the sheriff said. "But, do you ever? Sometimes I think that just knowing you from a distance is enough to get a man killed."

Jack did not like the sheriff's tone.

Does he have something on me he isn't sharing? Jack wondered.

Chapter 28
The ride back

"You guys take care now," the sheriff said loudly enough for Kate and the boys to hear. "I'll help you back that trailer up."

The sheriff then directed Jack backward past his marked patrol car and the garage to the point that he could steer his vehicle safely out onto M-123.

Jack, checking his mirror one last time, saw the sheriff just standing directly behind him, arms crossed and motionless. He waved to the sheriff in his mirror but did not receive a response.

The sheriff stood motionless until well after Jack had pulled south onto the highway, and then he set about re-securing the

Gordon house.

"What was *that* all about?" Kate asked. "I can't believe you broke the cup I bought for you."

"I just hope you can find another one just like it," Jack said with a grin.

"It was supposed to be unbreakable—double walled polycarbonate, or something like that. I bought it for you because it was made from the same material as bulletproof glass. And you broke it! I should have checked—you might have dropped it on a diamond."

"Well, that sure makes me feel good about bulletproof glass," Jack said with a chuckle. "At least you got the signal."

"I sure did," Kate said. "With an exclamation point."

"The sheriff was putting pressure on me," Jack continued, now *not* smiling. "They found my name and phone number on a piece of paper, in the car Festerman and Nacow had been driving. So the sheriff knew there was some sort of a connection to me."

"But that mug!" Kate chided. "I want you to know that it cost me thirty-five dollars. It wasn't a coffee-house giveaway. I wouldn't have said anything incriminating anyway."

"I'm sure you wouldn't have," Jack said. "But I couldn't take the chance."

"Do you think the sheriff knows about internal affairs flying out to talk to me?" Kate asked.

"Probably does," Jack replied. "But they would not have told him the nature of their visit. And besides, all they wanted to know about were the events surrounding Reg's death. And you were wounded, and then sedated. You had every reason not to remember anything."

"I actually don't remember much about it at all," Kate said. "I suppose I was in shock. What did you end up telling the sheriff about your connection to his two body bags?"

"The *truth,* of course. That Harold came up to go fishing with me and to introduce me to his protégé. He hoped I could put the young man in touch with some of my connections in New York. The stuff I told him was all true—just not *all* the truth."

Robby remained unusually quiet on the trip back to Sugar Island. But he was not sleeping.

Instead, he and Red were sitting in the back seats firing text messages back and forth in a wild frenzy.

"Okay, you two," she finally said. "What's got you guys so engrossed—video games or texting?"

"Red and I are planning our trip," Robby said.

Chapter 29

The trip

Trip? You boys are really planning on taking that trip?" she asked. "Before we go too far, the four of us have to make sure we are all on the same page. Where, exactly, are you going on this trip?"

"To the national forest," Robby answered. "We talked about it before. When I first asked about picking up my stuff."

"Okay, Father. I don't recall your telling me about giving these boys permission for any major expedition … into the *Black Forest*."

"No one gave us permission," Robby quickly countered, not wishing to create division between Jack and Kate. "You were there too. We kinda just talked about it. We just think that it will take more than one day—maybe three.

"It's really nothing that mysterious," Robby assured her. "It's just where my dad and I used to go camping—Hiawatha National Forest. And it's where *his* dad took him when he was my age. There're trails all through the forest, and the one we'll be using is well traveled. It's called the North Trail. It's west of Newberry."

"You're talking about the *western* section of the Hiawatha National Forest—the *western* section. Isn't that right?" Kate asked. "You'll need a ride way over there. That's on the other side of Munising."

"There's two parts to it," Robby answered. "The eastern section is located west and south of the Soo—that's where Dad and I used to go most of the time. But the part of it where Red and I need to go to is the western section. And it is pretty far. We could ride the bikes over there from the island, but a lift to the head of the North Trail would be nice."

"Hold on, here," Jack interjected with a grin. "Do you see what this kid just did to us? He's pretty slick. That's the second time he did that. He's a salesman. He assumed the sale by encouraging and accepting the secondary offer. He basically thanked us for the ride before we said he could even go. This kid's good. I'm going to have to keep my eye on him."

"You call it salesmanship. But it feels more like old-fashioned manipulation to me," Kate said, chuckling at her father's comment. "Was that what the map was for?"

"Yeah. It *was*."

"It *was*?" Jack asked. "I think I just detected the past tense of the verb. What does that mean?"

"The map is missing," Kate said.

"You couldn't find it?" Jack asked.

"Right," Robby said. "I had tucked it into my riding shoe, way down into the toe. And now it's gone."

"Are you sure you didn't hide it someplace else?" Jack asked.

"Before I went to camp with Red, I took the map out of the desk in my bedroom and wedged it down inside my riding shoe. Dad told me to hide it there. I knew I wouldn't be using those shoes until after I got back from camp. And, just in case my mom decided it was time to straighten up my room while I was camping, I didn't want her to put it someplace where I'd never find it. I'm positive I hid it in my shoes that I left at home. Dad was standing right beside me when I did it. It was one of the last times I talked to him."

"Anything else out of place? In your room?" Jack asked. "Or missing. Did you notice anything at all, besides the map, that was not where you'd left it?"

"Everything was moved around some," Robby said. "But nothing else was missing. At least, nothing that I noticed."

"Moved around, like you'd expect if your mom cleaned up your room?" Kate asked.

"Sort of," Robby said. "But it didn't look like she had cleaned the room. It was actually messier than I left it."

"But it didn't look tossed," Kate interjected. "If it had been thoroughly searched, it would have looked a lot worse than it did. I don't think the sheriff had it searched."

"Is it possible that your dad moved it?" Jack followed up. "After you'd left for camp?"

"He told me to put it there," Robby said. "He was with me when I stuck it in the shoe. And it wouldn't be something he would do."

"But, he could have taken it out *after* you left for camp?" Kate suggested.

"I suppose so. But I don't think he did."

"What makes you so certain?" Jack asked.

"My dad knew the map by heart," Robby said. "A few weeks before camp we were talking about it. He said that when I got back from camp, he and I would go exploring in the western region of Hiawatha. When I asked him if he could find it again without a map, he said he could blindfolded.

"We were sitting at the kitchen table when he drew it. He had a map that his father had drawn. It was wearing out, so he said he'd make a new one. Even though he had it laid out on the table, he didn't have to look at it when he drew the one for me.

"I think he wanted me to have a new map, one that was based on geocaching, not trees, rocks, and trails. We sat there, and he drew it out, right down to the number of yards off the North Trail … and landmarks. He knew them all."

"Could you find the location again, *without* a map?" Kate asked.

"I think so, if Red and I had enough time. I remember some of the landmarks and generally about how far to look off the trail. If we took shovels, a metal detector, and had a few days to poke around. It's been almost a year since he took me there, but I think we could find it. Especially with the Garmin."

"Garmin?" Jack asked.

"Listen to this," Kate said. "Robby's dad hid a homing device at the site. It gives off an electronic signal that his Garmin picks up when he gets close to it."

"A geocache with a Garmin chirper," Jack said. "You guys were really into this geocaching."

"So you know what he is talking about?" Kate asked.

"Sort of," Jack replied. "I've never done it, but it does sound intriguing. If there's a chirping device there, and if he knows about where the Geocache is hidden, the boys just might be successful. In fact, there's a very good chance that they will find it. As long as the battery in the chirper is still working. How long ago did he set up the chirper?"

"Months, a few months. Earlier this spring, after some of the snow had melted."

"Then it's still working," Jack said. "They're good for a year."

At that point, Red and Robby started to text about their anticipated adventure. In their minds, it was a sure thing.

Jack and Kate were not so certain.

Finally, Kate spoke up: "Well, Uncle Jack, are you ready to sign off on this one? It sounds like a ton of fun to me. If I didn't have some catching up to do, and if I adored snakes, I'd like to tag along. After all, what's the worst that could happen?"

Chapter 30

No stopping this train

The boys barely slept.

Even before Jack had a chance to grind his morning coffee beans, the two boys and Red's dog Buddy (a Golden Retriever) had begun preparation. They were intent on going exploring in the Hiawatha National Forest—Western Section.

When Jack reminded them that he and Kate had not yet fully discussed the trip—neither with them, nor with each other—they remained undaunted.

They correctly calculated that Jack would not have gone to the trouble of picking up the camping gear in the first place had he not intended to let them go exploring.

And Kate agreed. This was the first time she had seen Robby

begin to express himself openly since the murders of his mother and father. So, even though she had reservations about allowing the boys to go out on their own, she sensed the positives outweighed the negatives.

Besides, both Jack and Kate knew well Red's resourcefulness. He had, after all, fully fended for himself in the wild for nearly half of his life.

It was clear from the outset that all parties were confident that the trip was going to take place. What remained to be determined were the ground rules.

"Nice cup," Kate said to her father, noticing that he was drinking his coffee from a mug she had never seen before. "Where'd *that* come from?"

"Not sure," Jack replied. "It must have belonged to your Uncle Alex. I found it in that top cupboard, above the refrigerator."

Kate picked up the dark-colored handmade mug that her father was using and examined it more closely.

"Do you know what this is?" she asked.

"I have a pretty good idea," Jack admitted with a grin on his face. "It was the only one in the cupboard that I felt like taking with me on this trip—you know, after what happened yesterday."

"This masterpiece is in the shape of a naked woman," Kate chuckled.

"Really?" Jack offered incredulously. "Let me take a closer look at that. You know, I think you're right."

"I'm buying you a new unbreakable travel mug as soon as I get back to New York," she said.

"Sounds good to me," Jack said, standing to his feet to address the boys. "By unbreakable, I assume you mean more *unbreakable* than the last one—the one that was supposed to be bulletproof."

He picked up his coffee, wrapping his sizable hand around it, rather than holding it by the handle. "We are going to let you go on this *adventure*, but we are going to set some boundaries first. How well you handle these rules will determine whether or not we allow you to take trips in the future."

Robby had heard that speech before—from his father. But Red hadn't. Jack had never set many boundaries for Red, because he knew that the boy was going to do exactly what he wanted to do regardless of Jack's rules.

Even though he knew that Red was going to follow his own instincts and innate resourcefulness, still Jack was primarily addressing him. He hoped that Red would be the responsible one and watch out for Robby. While Jack was optimistic that Robby would be able to handle his freedom, he was counting on Red to maintain order and ensure their safety.

Even though Jack and Kate believed the boys were good kids, they knew that once their bikes hit the ground they were going to do pretty much as they pleased.

Jack covered some of the basics—never get separated, and always carry a compass, as well as a portable GPS. Have plenty of water and granola bars, and keep your cell phones handy.

The boys did their best to listen, but after a few of Jack's rules all they heard was Buddy's whining. He was anticipating something big. And he was right.

The boys texted constantly on the drive out to the trailhead. They had determined earlier to have Jack and Kate drop them off at Valley Spur. That was where Robby and his father had embarked on their earlier adventures in the forest.

While Valley Spur wasn't exactly the trailhead, it was the logical point from which to embark. From there they could ride their bikes west along the trails that laced through the forest. And when finished, they could return to that location for Jack to pick them up.

Not only did it have a restroom of sorts, but it provided adequate off-road parking for Jack and Kate to wait, just in case the boys were a little late.

"I will be back to pick you up at the trailhead tomorrow at dusk," Jack said.

The two boys looked at each other, and then Red started to text.

"Unk Jk. Hv slp bgs. 2 nts??"

Jack looked at Kate and showed her the text.

It was almost as though Kate saw this one coming. She shrugged her shoulders and said: "These kids are pros at this. I'd say give them an option."

She then turned and addressed the boys. "If by mid-afternoon tomorrow you still have not found the site, and if everything's okay, and if you have enough food, of course. Then call us and we will discuss it. But as it stands right now, your Uncle Jack and I will be here tomorrow at sunset to pick you up, right here at Valley Spur … same place we're dropping you off."

Red flashed a thumbs-up with a big smile.

Jack handed Red a cell phone charger as they were preparing to ride off. "Not sure why I'm doing this," he said. "I doubt that you will have coverage out there anyway. And if you do, I have no idea where you'd plug it in. But take it with you. It's light, and you just never know if it might come in handy. Keep your phones turned off until you're ready to use them. That way you should still have battery left through tomorrow."

"They'll probably have coverage in some places," Kate added.

Just as anticipated, as soon as the bicycles were unloaded, the boys were ready and eager to get going.

But before Red jumped on his bike, he ran over to Kate and gave her a hug, and then he hugged Jack.

Kate did not wait for Robby to do the same. He was already sitting on his bike, so she walked over and hugged him. Jack then wrapped his arm around Robby's neck from behind and gently flexed his muscle. "You guys take care of yourselves—okay?"

Even though Robby did not openly express his emotions, he made it clear by his silence that he appreciated the attention.

Jack and Kate watched the two Tom Sawyers ride off. Buddy, with tail wagging, brought up the rear.

Both boys had folding shovels strapped to their backpacks. Robby also had the metal detector attached to his, and it seemed to affect his balance, at least until he picked up a little speed.

While Red did offer up a blind but sincere wave as they rode off, neither boy looked back. They were intent on establishing separation between themselves and their adult caregivers.

Robby was clearly the leader at this point, largely because he had been hiking and riding in the national forest before.

He thought that if they crossed over M-94 right at Valley Spur, they could immediately catch Buck Bay Road.

That, he thought, would be the same route he and his father had taken before.

But it had been a long time, and he wasn't sure.

Chapter 31

The North Country Trail

For the first mile Buck Bay Road pretty much parallels the North Country Trail, also known as the NCT.

The boys planned to ride their bikes through the forest trails to see if Robby could get a fix on some of the landmarks he remembered from the missing map. They would use the established roads and snowmobile trails at first. And then, should they need to use the NCT, or venture out into the open forest, they would secure their bikes on one of the numerous gates that block off the old lumber trails.

Robby knew that bikes and motorized vehicles were banned from use on the NCT, so if they needed to traverse parts of that trail, they would have to leave their bikes behind.

To secure them, in that event, they had packed OnGuard Pitbull STD locks, which Robby's father had purchased for that purpose. "These locks will keep our bikes secure," he had said to his son. "A thief will need a high-speed battery-powered angle grinder to cut through them. It's not likely that'll happen."

If they found that they needed to cover more miles quickly, they could then return to their bikes and use them to follow some of the established truck and snowmobile trails.

While the North Country Trail is not always clearly marked in the forest, it is very well known. Running farther than any other hiking trail in the United States, it's known in books by its full name—the North Country National Scenic Trail. It begins in New York and ends in North Dakota, covering approximately three thousand, eight hundred miles.

About twenty miles of the trail passes through the Hiawatha National Forest, beginning at Munising Falls on the east and ending at Eben Road on the west.

It was off of this section of the trail that Robby believed he would find the stone formation discovered decades earlier by his father and grandfather.

Soon after the boys had disappeared around a curve and down a small hill, Kate said to her father, "Our work is done here, for now. But keep your cell on—we just might hear from them yet today."

As they fastened their seatbelts, Jack said, "I wonder if what we are doing falls under the category of 'child abuse'?"

Kate was not amused.

"Absolutely not," Kate responded. "I think CPS views it more as a case of child *neglect*."

While both Jack and Kate felt a little uneasy about granting the boys permission to go exploring on their own, especially with the possibility of extending it an extra day, they knew that had they denied Red and Robby the chance, the boys would have done it anyway.

Less than five minutes after they had disappeared into the forest, Robby jumped off his bike and ran off into the woods to pee.

"I gotta pee bad," he complained, fumbling with his zipper. "I would have used the toilet where your uncle dropped us off, but I was afraid he might change his mind about letting us stay two nights—so I just wanted to get going."

* * *

"The boys have stopped already," a man in a van parked nearby said to his partner as he fumbled around with an unfamiliar smartphone app. "I hope this works as advertised. Why would they have stopped?"

Chapter 32

I feel better

"That's better," Robby said. "That tree never had it so good."

Red texted: "Ht the Nrth trl?"

"It's north of here," Robby replied. "Some of these trails allow us to use the bikes—some don't. We'll get it figured out, and then move along. Our bikes are as safe locked up out here on one of these gates as they would be anyplace. There is a ton of activity around here. And standard bolt cutters won't faze these locks. You can't even use a hacksaw on them."

The gates Robby was referring to were installed years ago to block off the dozens of logging roads that slice through the woods. Were they not in place, those roads would be used for snowmobiles in the winter and ATVs in the summer. The gates do not actually control vehicular traffic, but they do discourage it.

"If someone has a high-speed grinder, he could cut the locks.

But those grinders are very loud. My dad has … *had* one. No one's gonna be pulling one of those puppies outta their backpack. Besides, there are just too many easier targets."

The two boys then headed west on Buck Bay Road.

* * *

"There," the man in the van said to his partner. "We've got both of them on the move again. Looks like they're headed west and north on Buck Bay. Just as we had hoped."

"But that still doesn't mean anything, not yet," his partner said.

Chapter 33

The hunt is on

It had rained the night before. Not a lot—just enough to soak the rich forest soil and release the million scents associated with this particular geographical area.

The boys had not gone far. They had ridden about three miles—from Valley Spur at M-94, past The Ponds Access, and were about fifty yards from Camp Au Train Road, also known as the Rapid River Truck Trail.

Red breathed in deeply. *I like this,* he thought. *It smells different from Sugar Island, but it's good.*

Robby, who had been leading the way, then stopped and turned to face Red. To this point, neither boy had pulled out the maps they had printed off the Internet the night before.

"Maybe we should go over this again," Robby said.

Both boys stopped and took off their backpacks. Placing them beside the trail, they each removed half a dozen printed sheets out of a latched pocket. Before sitting down on their backpacks to study the maps, they each retrieved a granola bar and a bottle of water from a separate compartment.

They weren't tired, lost, or hungry. They were celebrating their independence. They stopped and rested because they could. They had escaped the controls of the entire adult world and were totally alone and on their own—or so they thought.

Chapter 34

Hello world

"We're right here," Robby said, pointing to a spot on the map. "We are almost to Camp Au Train Road.

"That's sort of a road running north/south," he continued, redirecting his pointing finger up the trail. "Right over there."

The boys had gone over this many times the night before. Red had these first steps memorized. But because only one of them could talk, Robby pretty much carried both sides of the conversation.

It was their understanding that if Red had a specific thought he needed to express, he would interject it into their *conversation*, either with a text or some other type of nonverbal communication.

The boys' relationship was unusual. Robby was six months the senior—and he was slightly taller than Red. Given those two attributes, plus the fact that only Robby could talk, he would seem more likely to be the leader. But it didn't quite work out that way, at least when it came to decisions not based on Robby's knowledge regarding the specifics of his father's lost map.

Red had functioned so long on his own during the years before bonding with Jack and Kate that he had emerged as not a leader or follower. Red was independent.

Had he been able to talk, it is highly likely that he would take charge. But it was virtually impossible for him to exert authority without an acceptable way to communicate it.

So, Red found that he functioned best as a self-determining individual—at least with his peers.

Of course, when it came to Jack and Kate, Red recognized their authority and did his best to comply with their wishes—even when he did not want to. Most likely the father/son quasi-relationship he had formed through the years with Alex had instilled in him the ability to accept family structure. Alex had been, after all, not only Red's biological father, but he was also the brother of Jack's wife. Red probably sensed a familial affinity, even though he might not have recognized it as such.

But now that Red was attending school, and for the first time in years associating with children his own age, he found it difficult to lead or follow. If something seemed right to him, he would do it—if not, he walked away.

On this day, Robby was on a mission, and Red was his willing accomplice.

"Whts frst?" Red texted.

"I would like to ride north on Rapid River Truck Trail," Robby said.

"Why?" Red texted.

"I'm not real sure," Robby said. "I just remember that being on my dad's map for some reason. It's not where the rock formation is located, but I thought if we hit it for a mile or so, maybe I'd remember something about it. … You know, maybe I'd see some landmark that would tell me why it's significant."

"Cool lts go!" Red texted.

As the boys gathered up their litter and stuffed it into their backpacks, they heard a noise just ahead on the trail. They both stopped and stared in that direction. Buddy whined just enough to alert them.

Chapter 35

Rapid River

Two hikers, a man and a woman, were crossing Buck Bay Trail, headed north on Rapid River Truck Trail.

It looked to both Red and Robby that the couple had spotted them, because the woman appeared to glance in their direction more than one time. The boys did not move, and the couple kept going.

"Don't you think they saw us?" Robby asked.

Red did not bother to text. He simply scrunched up his mouth and nodded.

"Let's give them some time, and then we'll follow in behind them," Robby suggested.

The boys took off their backpacks again, laid them down, and sat on them.

And they waited.

* * *

"I guess that answers your question," the man said.

"Whaddya mean?"

"You saw them? Right? Over there, to the right—I think that's Buck Bay."

"Yeah, I saw them."

"Then it's safe to say our tracking devices are working. Looks like they're just taking a lunch break."

"Did you notice that they have that dog with them?"

"I did, do you think that will be a problem?"

"Not really. It's just something we have to keep in mind."

Chapter 36

Jack and Kate have their own challenges

Jack and Kate arrived at the Sugar Island Ferry in the early afternoon after dropping off the boys. As they were waiting for the final vehicles to drive off the ramp, they spotted a marked county car. And just as they suspected, it was the sheriff.

"Bet he's been out to see us," Kate said.

"He has my cell—he should just give me a call," Jack moaned.

Even though she knew that the sheriff had seen them in the line for boarding, she lowered her window and flagged him down.

The sheriff pulled in close and lowered his passenger window. "You guys headed back to the resort?" he asked.

"We are," Kate replied. "Would you care to join us for a cup of coffee? Dad makes the best coffee drinks."

"I would like that," the sheriff replied. "And maybe we can discuss a couple of other matters. If that'd be okay with you two."

"We should scoot," Kate said, realizing that she and Jack were holding up the line to board the ferry.

In almost any other place in the country, or perhaps in the world, someone would have impatiently blown his horn to move the line along. Even though their conversation was short, still every vehicle ahead of them had already boarded, and the crewman stood silently on the ramp waiting.

The sheriff glanced back at the ferry and then at the driver of the car directly behind Jack's. He smiled and waved. "That's just Jeffery, my insurance agent. I think he's got a thing for one of the bartenders at the Hilltop."

He then quickly inventoried all the vehicles remaining and said, "I should be able to get back on for this trip. I'll see you at the resort. And the coffee—that sounds great."

Jack nodded with a smile as he took his foot off the brake.

"I'll bet he takes his coffee black," Kate said. "Any idea why cops drink their coffee black? Is it in their genes?"

"Truck drivers are the same way—they like their coffee black as well," Jack said. "I think it's because if they spill it, it doesn't make such a big mess. It's hard to get the smell out of spilled milk or cream. So they just get into the habit of drinking it black."

"That's what I heard too," Kate agreed. "When I first got hired on I had to do patrol duty. I didn't drink coffee back then, but those who did always had it black."

The sheriff circled around and pulled into the line behind the last vehicle.

"I'm surprised that he didn't want to slide in ahead of us," Jack said with a smile. "I'll bet that if he didn't think he'd make the cut for this trip, that's exactly what he would have done."

Jack and Kate pulled onto the ramp and were directed into lane two. Jack was able to verify in his rearview mirror that all of the waiting vehicles, including the sheriff's, were able to fit on the ferry.

"It is amazing how many vehicles can be squeezed onto a ferry as small as the Sugar Island Ferry," Kate said. "I think it has a lot to do with the way Bill directs them on—compacts here, trucks there. I'll bet he does a great job packing the minivan for a family vacation."

They both agreed with Kate's assessment on Crewman Bill's talents, but then the conversation took a turn.

"What do you think he's got on his mind this time?" Kate asked.

Jack did not answer immediately. Instead, the two of them sat silently, pondering just what the sheriff might want to discuss with them.

And then Jack's cell phone began to vibrate.

Chapter 37

Hi, Pam

"Hi, Pam," Jack said, seeing that the call was from Pam, his friend (and Reginald Black's widow). "How are you?"

"I just got word that my two friends—Harold Festerman and David Nacow," Pam said. It was obvious that she was crying. "The authorities said that they had been murdered."

There was a long pause, but Jack did not interrupt her.

"Two officers stopped by my home," she continued. "They told me that the bodies of David and Harold had been found floating in the St. Mary's River, not far from Sugar Island. I'm assuming you know about that. Right?"

"Yes, the sheriff informed us that their bodies had been pulled out of the river," Jack said. "Were they *good* friends of yours?"

From the many years that Jack and her husband had worked together, Pam knew better than to say much on the phone. So she carefully guarded her words.

"Not *good* friends, but I would say that David was a friend. He and Reg used to talk a lot. David has been over to our house on occasion."

"I'm sure you know that Harold and I go back," Jack said, thinking it wise to take over the conversation just in case Pam did not exercise sufficient discretion.

"The three of us—Festerman, the young man, and I—we were planning to do some fishing up here. Plus, I think Harold wanted me to introduce his friend to some of my contacts in New York, which I would have been happy to do."

Jack then took the conversation into a whole new direction.

"Pam, Kate and I would like to have you come visit us at the resort, here on Sugar Island," he said. "It would be good for you, and for Kate as well. She could use a little female company. You two can go shopping at the new TJ Maxx here in the Soo, and all of the souvenir and ice cream shops will be open. How about it? If I make the reservations, will you come visit us?"

Pam knew Jack would not want to discuss anything of substance, sensitive or otherwise, over the phone, so the only way she would be able to discuss matters of importance with him would be for her to take him up on his offer.

So she thought about it for only a moment and then replied, "I'd love to get away. *And* I'd love to go shopping with Kate. I haven't seen her since the funeral ..."

Jack caught Pam's error. Kate had not been able to attend Reg's funeral. But he didn't correct her.

Pam's silence told Jack that she had begun crying again.

"Which airport would you like to use—Kennedy or LaGuardia?" Jack asked.

Pam thought for a bit and then said, "LaGuardia would be

more convenient, but either would work. I would prefer not to have a flight out of Newark, though. The taxi fee would be a killer."

"I'm sure I can find something out of LaGuardia," he said, glancing over at Kate to have her start searching on her iPad.

"Shall we make it for a week?" Jack asked. "How long would you *like* to stay?"

"That's too long," she said. "You'll get really sick of me by then."

"Nonsense," Jack responded. "I'll reserve the best unit available at the resort. You'll love it. We can catch up on old times. It'll be fun. My only concern is whether you can get away for that long. Will a week work?"

"A week would be great," Pam replied. "I've had no vacation since Reg passed away. It's been very tough. … I know you two were the best of friends. He spoke so highly of you. He loved you more than anyone, except for me, of course. We were best friends. Jack, I can't tell you how hard it's been."

Jack, not wanting the conversation to get personal, felt it necessary to end with those thoughts.

"Pam, I've got to go now. I *have* to. Kate is online right now making arrangements for your visit. I'll have her email you with her recommendations. Just know that we are both eager to spend some time with you. Even under these circumstances, it'll be fun having you visit. Love ya."

"Love ya too, Jack," Pam said. "And thanks. And give Kate a big hug for me."

"Will do," Jack said. "Gotta go now."

Chapter 38

Unlike two ships

The boys waited about twenty minutes. Both were getting anxious.

Finally, Robby spoke up: "I think we've waited long enough. Don't you?"

Red flashed a thumbs-up as he stood to his feet and began pulling his backpack over his shoulder.

"They didn't look like they were in any kind of a hurry, so we might be running into them on the trail. But that's okay. At least we can get a good look at the trail, for future use."

Buddy was ready to move on.

"Dz anytng lk fmlr?" Red texted.

"No. But I didn't expect it would. I'm thinking that this trail might be significant in some other way. Like maybe it connects to something else. Or, maybe there's a power line running across it, and that it might help us access something else. Dad noted it for some reason. We can check it out for a mile or so, and if nothing pops out at me, at least we will know what's up there."

Just then Buddy sounded his quiet alert once again—and for a good reason.

About one hundred yards ahead and moving toward them were the same two hikers that they had seen passing by about forty-five minutes earlier.

"Looks like we're gonna get a close-up look at these guys this time—they're headed right toward us."

But the hikers did not wait to meet the boys. They found the first clearing and headed off to the west.

Chapter 39
Now this is interesting

Looks like we scared them off," Robby said glibly, unable to get a read as to why the couple sought to avoid them.

When Robby looked back, Red flashed him an affected smile indicating that he was confused as well.

Buddy could not have cared less. He was just happy to be with his two best friends.

The boys rode until they came across an old dismantled railroad track. That was what Robby was looking for.

He had remembered his father explaining that until a few years earlier the rails remained on the ties, even though no trains actually traveled along this section of the Duluth South Shore and Atlantic Railway system.

With the steel rails and wood ties removed, rail cars loaded with lumber had since given way to snowmobiles, ATVs, mountain bikes, and motorcycles—and, of course, hikers.

Once Robby had satisfied himself that he and Red were, indeed, on the trail that crossed the old railroad, he knew that if they returned to the road they had come in on and turned west on it, eventually it would wind around and lead them to within a mile or so of the sought-after rock formation.

The boys decided that it would be good to take another rest stop. While they had not ridden very far, their heavy backpacks and the looseness of the gravel on the road had tired them out.

Not only that, but the mere fact that they were totally on their own made resting when they wanted to seem even more desirable.

After a granola bar and a bottle of water, Robby explained the history of the area to Red.

During the '30s and early '40s, before World War II, men ages eighteen to thirty-two were hired by the federal government under the auspices of the Civilian Conservation Corps (CCC) to harvest large quantities of lumber from Michigan's upper and lower peninsulas, as well as in various other rural areas throughout the United States.

Their duties consisted of much more than merely cutting down trees. They also replanted forests that had already been harvested, built hundreds of parks, constructed or built hundreds of miles of new roads, and performed numerous other worthwhile tasks that improved conservation.

For their efforts, they were paid thirty dollars per month by the federal government, twenty-five of which they were required to send back to their parents.

In the part of the Hiawatha National Forest where Robby and Red were biking, the CCC was charged with the job of replanting the forest that had earlier been harvested.

Robby explained to Red that if the boys were to continue south on the Rapid River Truck Trail (which is the road on which they encountered the mysterious couple), past Buck Bay Road (which is the road they came in on), after about one mile they would cross the North Country Trail.

When Robby said that, Red started to text. But Robby stopped him.

"I know what you're thinking," Robby said. "But there is a good reason why we need to head west on Buck Bay Road."

And then Robby went on to clarify why the longer way was actually the quicker way.

Robby had said earlier that the stone formation that they were seeking was located in a remote area directly south of the NCT but not terribly far from it.

The reason Robby was leading them on a route substantially north of the NCT was that they would not be permitted to ride their bikes on the NCT. He had explained that earlier to Red and Jack, but Red had forgotten.

As soon as Robby reminded him about that rule, Red recalled the previous conversation.

Robby was delighted to spell the whole thing out to Red as they sat there on their backpacks. It was exactly how Robby's father described his experience when he and Robby's grandfather had shared a similar adventure decades before. In fact, Robby suspected that this might even be the exact place he and his father had this talk.

Had it been possible, Robby might have lit up a cigar as he pontificated, because that is what his father did on their trip. Instead, Robby peeled the wrapping off another granola bar, but only after he had handed one to Red and poured out some water for Buddy.

Chapter 40
Sheriff Green's Inquiring mind

"Bring back memories, Sheriff?" Kate asked, not sure if Sheriff Green would figure out what she was getting at.

The sheriff thought for a moment and then replied, "Not yet. Maybe once your dad makes me a double espresso, with a whipped cream crown to keep the heat in. Maybe then I'll remember what you're talking about."

"I thought you'd be a *black* coffee drinker," Kate replied.

What Kate was hinting at with her *bring back memories* comment was what had transpired the first time she had met the sheriff. Jack and she were trying to solve the murder of her Uncle Alex, and during the course of their investigation they walked into a small coffee shop in Sault Ste. Marie.

The owner of the coffee shop was Joey, and he was a friend of Deputy Bill Green—later to become *Sheriff* Bill Green.

Deputy Green was sitting at the end of the bar at Joey's Coffee Shop when Jack and Kate walked in. Initially, Deputy Bill just sat there silently—listening intently to the conversation between Jack and Joey, slowly nursing his cup of black coffee.

Kate had delicately brought up their original encounter to serve as a reminder to the sheriff that one of his good friends, Joey the coffee guy, was deeply involved in the art heist that ultimately led to the murder of Alex, Kate's uncle.

Realizing that from time to time Sheriff Bill would throw it in Kate's and Jack's faces that they were involved in the death of the former sheriff (the one he replaced), Kate wanted to remind Sheriff Bill that one of his good friends was not only an art thief, but also a murderer.

"You've got a great memory," he chuckled. "But you're right. When I was on the road I always drank my espressos black—that is, when I could get espressos on the road. And when I was jawing with my friends at the coffee shop, it was always a shot-in-the-dark—Joey gave me free refills."

Kate pulled up a chair for the sheriff to join them at a small table where Jack and she usually ate breakfast.

The walls, painted in a soft white, featured primarily original watercolor works of local Native American artists.

The art was a holdover from before the murder of Alex, the previous owner of the resort. It was he, Alex, who had left the resort to Kate in his will. Both Jack and Kate knew that Alex was actually Red's biological father, but neither of them knew that Red's mother, Alex's secretary, had picked out all the wall hangings as well as most of the furniture. Red was aware that his mother had decorated the apartment. And it was largely because of his fondness of the provincial décor that the Handlers had decided not to redecorate—at least not at that time.

The sheriff sat facing the large window that overlooked the St. Mary's River. For a few moments, he said nothing. And neither did the Handlers. Instead, the sheriff just stared at the pier and the fishing boats tethered to it. The wispy limbs of a neatly trimmed weeping willow framed the scene on the top, and a perfectly coiffured lawn adorned the foreground.

Jack, still preparing coffee, allowed his eyes to meet Kate's as they waited for the sheriff to talk.

Jack clicked on the heat to the espresso maker and was grinding some dark roast.

"And still, when I'm on the road," the sheriff replied, "I drink it black. But, today, when I'm sitting down with my good friends, I like a little sweet with it."

Good friends, Jack repeated in his mind as he shook a can of whipped cream. *Wonder what the sheriff is after today?*

Jack handed the sheriff a doppio con panna—that is a double espresso with a shot of whipped cream.

Sheriff Green took a short sip of the very hot drink, and he smiled his approval.

"Times, now, are very different, at least for me they are," the sheriff said. "Things are going on up here. *Bad* things."

Chapter 41
A simpler time

In many ways, those were simpler times, back then," the sheriff continued, as he took the napkin next to his cup and wiped some whipped cream off his face. He sighed, leaned back on his chair, and thought of when he had less responsibility, less on-call time, more family time.

His kids were growing up too fast, and he regretted missing too many basketball games, Christmas programs, and church services.

With unemployment over ten percent, crime was on the increase. This made his job even more demanding. While he loved serving the thirty-nine thousand good people of Chippewa County, he was beginning to resent the sacrifice.

"Back in those days life was so much easier for me. I could just go over to Joey's little coffee shop and dump all my troubles on him. Of course, Kate, little did I know he was using me. Actually, the sheriff, Sheriff Northrup, was using him to get to me, to find out what I knew, and what his deputies were talking about."

"I know what you mean," Kate agreed. "Friendships, relationships of any type, don't function well when one or more of the parties are exercising agendas. I've found that you can't always spot the person with an agenda—at least not right away.

"But eventually it becomes apparent. And when it does, when you get confronted with the knowledge that someone you liked and respected was playing you. You learn from it. And move on. That's one positive thing that can emerge from that sort of a dysfunctional relationship. You learn to avoid it the next time. Or, at least you try to."

All of a sudden Kate recognized what she was doing.

Oh my God, she thought. *Here I am warning the sheriff about people with agendas, and I have an ulterior motive myself!*

Kate's *agenda* was to coax the sheriff into a greater level of transparency when relating to her and her father. She was trying to help the sheriff express himself with candor.

She was about to find out whether her efforts were going to work. She looked closely at him—his short neatly cut dark hair had started to turn gray around the temples. He was always clean-shaven. His coffee-colored brown uniform with the tan tie was impeccable, and his boots were always polished, military style.

His one drawback, Kate felt, was that he wore too much cologne. She thought it was 1970s English Leather. While that was a distraction, she knew it was not her job to fix it. *His wife can't be pleased with his using cologne like that.*

She felt his new responsibilities had aged him during the past few months, with deep creases in his face and a sadness in his brown eyes.

"Well, Kate, I think my best approach here would be to tell you what I know and ask you to comment on it, perhaps clarify some issues that are troubling me. Can I count on you, both of you, to help me? That is, if you're able?"

"Sheriff," Kate responded, "I will talk to you about anything that does not involve the violation of confidences. I will assure you that I will not lie. And I won't parse words. And I know my father feels the same way."

Kate sat next to him with her own coffee. Wearing a white, freshly pressed shirt and skinny jeans, she leaned into him, almost whispering, to get his attention, "If you bring up a matter that I am not comfortable discussing, I will tell you that. And you can then choose to press it, or move away. But I promise that I will not lie or mislead. Is that acceptable?" She then folded her hands together in front of her on the table, much like a chess player waiting for her opponent to make the next move.

"Let me start by informing you that I talked to your boss today—Captain Spencer. Nice guy. And he has the utmost respect and admiration for you."

"I suppose you had your reasons to contact him." Kate sighed.

"Being that the latest bodies that have turned up in my county were acquaintances of your father, and at least one of them was from the city where you work, I didn't think it'd be a stretch to see if he knew anything."

"And did he?" Her eyes narrowed.

"Not really. But he did tell me that internal affairs had recently sent an attorney to get a deposition from you regarding the death of one of your friends—Mr. Reginald Black. I understand that Mr. Black was also an associate of your father's. Is that correct?"

"Correct on both counts," she replied matter-of-factly.

"Would you tell me why internal affairs wanted to put you under oath and what they wanted to know?"

Kate unfolded her hands and put them flat on the table. Looking disgustedly at her unpolished nails, she finally allowed her eyes to focus on the gold ring with a lapis-lazuli setting that she always wore on her right hand. It had been her mother's favorite piece of jewelry. In moments such as this, it gave her a sense of strength and fortitude.

"Anytime IA puts a law enforcement officer under oath, it is prudent to have an attorney present when dealing with it. I did so at that deposition, and she has advised me not to discuss the contents of that deposition with anyone. So I can't really discuss it with you. But, I will say this about that interview. It happened. It lasted less than fifteen minutes. The only questions they asked me had to do with what I remembered about the night Reg, Mr. Black, was shot. I will tell you the same thing I told the lawyer. I had been kidnapped and held against my will. Reg rescued me, at least as far as I know he did. I have no actual memory of the event. I was shot. And as I've heard, Reg was shot as well."

She took a minute to look away and glance at Jack at the other side of the table from her. He sipped his coffee and looked over his cup, his eyes focused on hers with a hint of support, letting her know she was going in the right direction.

It was hard for her to bring back that period in her life. It had been a horrible experience, one from which she barely escaped with her life.

"Fortunately for me, my wound was much less serious than his. I was told later that he died. The lawyer asked me more questions, but my answer was always the same. I simply don't know anything else beyond that. I just don't remember."

Kate uncrossed her legs at that point, subconsciously preparing to walk out of the door and breathe in some Sugar Island fresh air. But the questioning continued.

"Do you know anything about his widow? I think her name is Pam?" the Sheriff asked.

"Both Pam Black and her late husband, Reg, are long-time friends of my father's. Through the years, Dad and Reg worked cases together, but that was all confidential, and Dad did not talk about them to me. I understand that Reg saved my life and ended up dead as a result of it. Because of that, the Blacks hold a very special place in my heart."

"What do you know about certain parties seeking to exhume Mr. Black's body?"

Kate did not want to talk about that. Jack considered jumping into the conversation but thought better of it. He was certain that Kate would handle it well.

Kate cleared her throat, sipped the coffee, and continued, "The truth is, Sheriff, Pam and my father have discussed that matter. She has not discussed it with me. So I would defer to him on that matter."

"Okay, Jack." The sheriff turned his chair a bit to look him in the eye. "Are you willing to talk to me about that exhumation issue?"

Both Jack and the sheriff knew that this conversation could get sticky if not handled properly. While most private detectives will hold confidential all information provided them by a client, if law enforcement obtains a subpoena, the private investigator is required to reveal the name of his client and the information called for in the subpoena. In other words, the attorney-client privilege, as is protected under federal case law, is not summarily extended to cover private investigators and their clients.

That having been stated, in most cases law enforcement will not press the issue because they know that if they really intend to force a private investigator to talk when he doesn't want to, they will need an appropriate subpoena.

"Sheriff," Jack replied. "You and I both know that there is no real right for confidentiality extended to a private detective and his client. But there is such a thing as propriety. I would like you to respect the propriety of relationship between myself and my clients."

"Are you saying that you work for Pam Black in that capacity?" the sheriff asked.

"Pam and I are old friends, and you would be correct in assuming that she is a client."

"Would you have a problem if I talked to her directly?"

"Absolutely not," Jack replied. "In fact, I would be happy to set up a meeting. Pam is flying out to meet with me in the very near future. When she arrives, I will let you know, and if she is willing to do so, I will have her talk to you."

The sheriff thought about it for a few moments and then asked, "Then am I correct in thinking that you are going to *encourage* her to talk to me? Is that what you are suggesting?"

"That's exactly correct," Jack said. "Of course, I would like to be present, if that is okay with you."

"I'd have no problem with that," the sheriff said. "She'd probably be more comfortable with you by her side, anyway. I'm assuming that she will also have an attorney present. Is that correct?"

"I will ask her if she wants to have an attorney. That would be her choice. Obviously, she has a right to an attorney. I'm not sure what she will want to do in that regard. Certainly you'd have no objection to that, would you?"

Chapter 42

The Rommel story

"Well," Robby said. "The story goes that just about where this road, the Rapid River Truck Trail, crosses the NCT, there is an old camp. It dates from the mid-1940s—right after World War II. Actually it dates much earlier than that, because it was originally built by the CCC.

"But after World War II it took on a different purpose. It was used to house German prisoners of war—a couple hundred of Rommel's troops were held there after they were captured in Africa. My dad said Rommel was a very popular German general. They called him the 'Desert Fox.'

"Anyway, it is quite possible, my dad told me, that German prisoners of war walked on these very roads. And that from time to time, some of them escaped. Who knows? We might actually run into one of their descendants."

With that, Red started to laugh. Both boys were thinking the same thing: maybe the couple that they had run into were the grandchildren of an escaped German prisoner, and they were worried about getting caught.

Of course, they both recognized the absurdity of that thought, but it was still good for a chuckle.

Then Robby, in his best imitation of his father, shared one more tidbit of conjecture that he had learned on his earlier adventure to the forest.

His father had told him that the old CCC camp, the one used by the military to house the German prisoners of war, was known as Camp Au Train. And that the camp might not be where commonly thought. That is, it might not be located where the NCT crosses Rapid River Truck Trail, as is indicated on most maps.

His father had told him that the actual location of the camp is more likely to be closer to the Coalwood Trail railroad tracks, which is well south of NCT—very close, in fact, to M-94.

His father had determined that on the basis of the coordinates he had found on a geocaching website.

"Dad thought that it is more likely that the CCC camp would be located close to the railroad tracks," Robby said.

"But the fact is," he continued, "the maps list the location about one-half mile north. But who knows?"

Robby loved to talk to Red, and Red loved to listen. But at that point, both boys knew it was time to move on.

The rest had been beneficial. And so had the sugar in the granola bars. The two boys covered the three miles from the old railroad trail back to Buck Bay Road in half the time it had taken them to get there.

Robby, still leading the way, barely slowed down as he turned west on Buck Bay Road.

Red was right behind him.

The thoughts about the mysterious couple had been totally overwhelmed by the stories of runaway German prisoners of war and the American soldiers who might still be chasing them down.

It was getting close to noon. They had not yet discussed where they would camp for the night.

Finally, after they had ridden nearly a mile west on Buck Bay Road, Red let out a growl.

Robby knew what that meant. Red wanted to stop.

Red rode his bike up beside Robby and pulled out his cell phone. After noticing that he did not have service, he put it back and unfolded a map.

Carefully he traced his finger along Buck Bay Road to a point just before the bridge that crossed the Au Train River.

At that point, he traced the road that runs straight north. Robby immediately realized what he was suggesting. About one mile north of Buck Bay Road was a campground. That would be the perfect place to pitch their tents. They could rest up for the night and then head south toward the location of the stone formation first thing in the morning.

"That's exactly what I had in mind too," he said. "We'll get up there early to mid-afternoon, and then we can get an early start in the morning."

When they arrived they discovered that there was a fee to camp in the campground. That would not have been a problem, because the boys had money.

But they knew they would not be permitted to camp there without adult supervision.

“I’ll take care of this,” Robby quickly remarked. “Just follow me.”

Chapter 43

Sheriff Green happy

It was all set. Sheriff Green was going to get the chance to talk directly to Pam Black when she came out to visit Jack.

The sheriff did not like the idea of poking around in Jack's business. But he had two murders to solve, and they seemed to lead right back to Jack and his associate—Pam Black. The sheriff felt he had no choice. If he were ever going to get to the bottom of those murders, he would have to talk to the person for whom the victims were working.

As was his practice, Jack abruptly ended the meeting.

Almost like a soldier snapping to attention when a ranking officer walked in the room, Jack sprang to his feet, pushing his chair slightly as the back of his knees struck it.

All of the chairs at this table were office style, with substantial padding, arms, a height-adjustment lever, and five wheels. Jack selected this style of chair because he did a lot of work at that table and he liked the comfort this type of chair provided.

The sheriff got the message. He knew that the meeting was over and that it was time for him to leave.

"It was really nice to talk to you," Jack said with a sincere smile as he led the sheriff toward the door. "As soon as Kate has finalized the plans for Pam's visit, we'll let you know. Right now we have no idea how long she will be in town or exactly when. But, we will get in touch with you when we do."

The sheriff shook Jack's outstretched hand and thanked him for the coffee. Kate also walked up and extended her hand, which the sheriff promptly also shook.

Kate knew that she needed to allow the sheriff a proper means of excusing himself, but she was made a little uncomfortable when the sheriff placed his hand on Jack's shoulder. She never encouraged that degree of familiarity with co-workers, or with superiors.

The handshake worked, and the sheriff headed toward his car not only happy with the results the meeting produced, but glad also to have left Jack's company. Jack intimidated him.

"That could have gotten interesting," Kate said once the door had closed.

"It certainly could have," Jack agreed. "I'm glad that he didn't try to push it. He might not be polished, but he's beginning to learn the ropes."

Kate removed the cups from the table and headed toward the sink with them.

Jack intercepted her on the way and snatched his red cup of now-cold coffee.

"I think I'll warm this up a bit," he said.

"I know what that means," Kate chuckled. "You're not finished with the Reg thing, are you?"

"No, not really," Jack said. "I'll run some of this by Roger. He's got chips on the table too. Maybe he has a different take. Or, maybe he has some info we don't have.

"And there's one other very nice thing about talking to Roger. His phone is never monitored by the NSA, or anyone else. That's a rare gift these days."

"How can you be so sure about that?" Kate asked. "They've been monitoring foreign leaders, embassies, and just about everything else. Why not Roger's phone?"

"He assures me," Jack replied, "that as a senior officer in the Secret Service, his phone is off limits to the NSA, and it's encrypted as well. Roger just doesn't get that stuff wrong. If he says it's secure, it is secure. My end too, as long as I stay off landlines."

"Hey, Rog."

"Jack, how's it going?"

"Great. Just great. And you?"

"You did not call to exchange pleasantries. What's on your mind?"

"I just got off the phone with Pam Black," Jack said. "She's flying out to visit us shortly."

"And to talk to you about that exhumation business?" Roger asked.

"Yeah. She's not sure which way to turn on this one. Allison is not going to give it up."

"And she won't," Roger responded. "She is totally determined to press ahead on this thing. I'm afraid the best thing Pam can do is to give it her blessing."

"It must be the money," Jack said. "Don't you think?"

"I would," Roger said. "She must be getting some advice along that line, maybe from her husband. They've been meeting more frequently lately. I think it might have to do with that. At least in part."

Jack paused and then asked, "What might the other part be?"

Jack knew that Roger currently served on Allison's Secret Service detail—in fact, he had been the head of her detail since her husband left office. Jack also knew that Roger should not be talking to him about any matters relating to Allison.

Roger hesitated before responding to Jack's question.

After an uncomfortable silence, Jack rephrased his question.

"Everyone knows that Allison is putting an organization together to give herself another shot at the presidency. And it is also common knowledge that her husband is one of the greatest political minds of this generation. Hell, if I were thinking about running for president, the first person I would want on my side would be Bob Fulbright. It would just make sense. So, I would assume that she would seek out her husband's help in putting her strategy together."

"That would make sense," Roger said. "If *you* were running for president I suspect that is exactly what *you* should do.

"And everyone knows that it takes a hell of a lot of money to make a run," Roger quickly added. "More now than ever before—

possibly as much as a billion."

"The only way that I can see this exhumation business paying off for her," Jack said, "is if she suspects that she might find some sort of clue on Reg's body as to where he might have stashed the gold that she gave him to plot and carry out … to fulfill the terms of that very important contract."

Even though Jack knew that Roger was aware that Allison had hired Reg and Jack to assassinate the president, he still did not want to utter the word "assassination."

"I know what you mean," Roger said. "But this is the most secure connection available on the planet. My friends at Mossad developed this system, and it *is* secure. It is the same encryption used by Netanyahu. And he's probably the only world leader not hacked by the NSA. Hell, Allison and Bob are on it as well."

"If you're comfortable, I'm comfortable," Jack said.

"When did you say you were going to be meeting with Pam?" Roger asked.

"Not sure yet, but quite soon."

Roger paused for a long moment. "There is someone I think you should talk to before you meet with her. He's been bugging me to talk to you. Can you hang on until I see if I can get hold of him?"

"Sure," Jack said. "I'm just warming up my coffee. I'll set my phone down while I get it out of the microwave. Okay?"

Jack walked over to the microwave and removed his coffee. Kate had washed out the cups and wiped down the coffeemaker.

"Mind if I stick around for this?" she said. "Or would it be best if I didn't hear your end?"

"Plausible deniability," Jack advised with a smile.

"I'll be back," she said. "Just going to freshen up."

Jack walked back to the table with his hot coffee and picked up the phone.

"Rog," he said. "I'm back."

"Jack?" the voice on the phone said. "Is that you?"

There was a long pause as Jack registered what he had just heard.

"Reg!" Jack exclaimed. "Reginald Black! Is that *really* you?"

Chapter 44

Finding the right adult

The boys rode through the camp until they found just the right campers.

"Hey," Robby said to a twenty-five-year-old bearded man who was standing beside a fairly beat-up smaller motorhome. "How ya doin'?"

They exchanged greetings, and then Robby said, "My friend and I need a place to pitch our tents for the night. We can't get in, officially, without our parents being here. Do you think you could let us share your spot, right behind your camper, if I gave you ten bucks?"

"How about twenty?"

"Sounds good," Robby said, handing the man a twenty-dollar bill. "I promise we won't be any trouble to you. And we'll be outta your hair when the sun comes up."

"That's cool," the man replied. "We're gonna be fishing at sunrise anyway. You won't be bothering us. For another twenty you can stay two nights."

Red and Robby looked at each other. Red shrugged his shoulders, signaling his agreement, and Robby gave the man a second twenty.

"Just don't be making noise at night," the bearded man said. "I like it quiet when I sleep."

"No problem," Robby agreed.

Just before the man turned, Red handed Robby the cell phone charger Jack had given him.

"Oh, and would it be okay if we used your power to charge our cells tonight?" Robby asked.

"No problem. There's a power outlet right on the back of the camper. Feel free."

The boys were excited that their trip was going so well. They'd get up in the morning, head south until they could ride their bikes no longer, lock them up onto something substantial, and hike on from there.

They had high hopes that they would find what they were looking for, and then they could head back for the night.

If they needed more time to search for evidence proving European Bronze Age visitors, then they would tackle it again for a few hours on their last morning.

Finally, they would grab their bikes and burn it back to Valley Spur to meet up with Jack and Kate.

But they were not the only ones basking in success. Two campsites down from them was parked a one-hundred-thousand-dollar motor home. The boys had admired it when they rode in on their bikes.

In fact, as they passed by, Robby snickered, "Stay away from those snobs. They'd turn us in and get us kicked out of the campground."

Inside that motor home were a man and a woman, and they were intently monitoring everything Red and Robby were doing.

Chapter 45

What does Pam know about this?

Kate busied herself in her office while Jack talked to Roger and the mysterious third party. She knew that her father would share with her any information that he calculated would not jeopardize her position in some future litigation, particularly that which might affect her career.

After about ten minutes, Jack pulled up a chair in Kate's office and sat down facing her.

Kate turned to face him.

"Well," Jack said, carefully weighing his words. "This business is getting complicated. I want you to listen very carefully to every word I say. Feel free to read into them as you see fit. But don't interrupt, and don't ask me to explain anything."

"This really sounds intriguing," Kate said with a smile. "I think you're telling me that this is *not* a game of 'twenty questions'?"

"Exactly," Jack replied. "Here's the deal. At least as much of the deal as I dare reveal at this time.

"Roger is totally aware of Allison's enthusiasm with regard to exhuming Reg's body from Calvary Cemetery. … And, he is also totally aware of what is prompting it. Now remember, Kate, do not interrupt to ask follow-ups, no matter how strong the urge.

"I will let you know when this conversation is finished. And when it is, it will not be revisited, at least not at this time."

Kate, the homicide detective, watched him very carefully and was already beginning to figure out where her father was going, particularly with regard to the part where he told her to be prepared to read into his words meanings he would not be expressing.

"Roger set up a conference call with an *interested* third party," Jack said. "That's when I asked you to leave the room."

As soon as Jack mentioned that there was an "interested third party," Kate began a process of elimination to determine whom that third party might be. Three names came to mind.

For a moment, she tuned her father out and began running the possibilities through her mind.

He could be talking about Pam. She fits that description. But she's coming out to meet with us. If Dad had just been talking to her, he would have said so.

Maybe it's Allison. That is a real possibility. Allison is a principal player, and Roger is on her security detail. He would have ample access to her. Could be Allison.

And it could be, based on the level of secrecy Dad is exercising, it just could be Reg himself. He's supposed to be dead. So that would be really weird. But stranger things have happened, especially in New York.

Jack observed that Kate was staring unfocused over his shoulder. He knew that when she did this she was deep in thought. So he stopped talking until she looked back into his eyes.

"Now, the *man* that Roger had me talk to—" Jack said.

That answered her question. Kate now knew that Reginald did not die from his gunshot wound. At that point it all began to make sense to her.

Roger had handled all the arrangements at Reg's death. She knew that to have been the case because, even though her wounds had prevented her from attending the funeral, her father had later described it all to her. Jack had told her at the time that Reginald had succumbed to a heart attack. That did sound a little strange to her, but she knew better than to press the issue.

The notion of plausible deniability was a common theme in her father's thinking. He had often told her that the less she knew for a fact about certain matters, the safer she would be.

Momentarily forgetting what her father had instructed regarding interrupting with questions, Kate asked, "When Pam comes out, will she have knowledge of this man you just talked to?"

Instead of answering her question, Jack just smiled and asked, "How are you coming with her travel plans?"

Chapter 46
Sleeping well

The boys slept well that night—probably because they had so thoroughly worn themselves out riding their bikes.

They arose bright and early, broke camp and packed up their tents. Even though they would have liked a shower, they knew better than to hang around too long.

Red pulled out his cell phone and checked for coverage. But he still had none.

Robby saw what he was doing and knew the reason: Red wanted to find out what Robby had planned for the day.

"Let's get started before someone starts asking us questions," Robby said, as he adjusted the straps on his backpack. They had cut into his neck the day before, so he made sure he tucked some padding between the strap and his shoulder.

Red was fine with his backpack from the day before. But that was not due to any additional padding on his straps. His burden was simply lighter than Robby's because he was not carrying the metal detector. He had offered several times to help out with it, but Robby insisted on dealing with that additional piece of equipment.

As the two boys headed south on Campground Road, the man in the expensive motorhome asked the woman with him, "Shall we break out the Gators today? Or follow on foot?"

Attached to the back of their forty-five-foot motorhome was a twenty-foot enclosed trailer containing two John Deere Gators.

Chapter 47

Day two

When the boys reached Buck Bay Road, they stopped.

"If we have time before we leave," Robby said, "Maybe we can take a ride across the bridge over the Au Train River, and then south on Au Train Forest Lake Road—it's kinda cool. There's a neat little waterfall down by the electrical plant.

"But for today, we need to see about finding that stone formation. And it's accessible best from the east side of the river.

"We'll head east on Buck Bay Road. We've been there before. That's the way we came in. But instead of heading all the way back on it, we'll catch it right up here in about three-quarters of a mile.

"That would be County Road 531. Also known as USFS 2482.

We will head south on that road for almost three miles.

"At some point along there we will need to ditch our bikes and go on foot. A lot of those old lumber roads are blocked off with heavy-duty steel gates. We should be able to lock our bikes onto one of them. We'll log the coordinates so we can find them when we want to."

Red smiled. Robby knew exactly what Red was thinking.

"Yeah. It would sure help if we had the coordinates of that stone formation—it would make finding it a ton easier.

"But even without them, I think I can get us in pretty close using my memory of landmarks. And from there we can follow the geocaching chirp beacon.

"This time we'll keep a record of its location. I'll email you and me the coordinates, in a code. That's how we do it. We use simple cryptograms for that.

"That's what my dad did on his map. He sketched out a little map and then listed the coordinates in code, along with an enciphered clue. Too bad it's gone. But maybe that's good. It makes it more exciting—more of a challenge.

"All we have to do is get close—to within thirty feet. I think I can do that. Dad programmed it to tell me where the actual formation is located. When we hear the chirp—we're in."

Red then pulled out his cell phone but still had no service. So he just held it so that Robby could read what he was texting.

"U wth hm whn he hid the Chrp?"

"Yeah," Robby said. "But I didn't pay a lot of attention. I thought he'd be coming back with me. Plus it was getting dark. We'd waited a little too long to leave. I guess we were having too much fun. I was with him, but my memory is a little foggy. I think if we can get in the general vicinity, I can find it. The battery should last a year or more, and it hasn't quite been a year.

"I do remember that Dad hid the chirp about one hundred yards from the rock formation. But he provided pretty specific directions on it. I'm pretty sure I can find the chirp."

What Robby was not aware of was that the person who had stolen the map from his shoe had ventured out into the Hiawatha National Forest and, with the help of the map, had located the chirping device.

Chapter 48 The monkey wrench

Then, following the directions provided by the chirp, the thieves entered a thicket not far from it. After poking around in the thick brush, they eventually located the rock formation that was so important to the elder Gordon, and then they removed the geocache that marked the find.

They then decided that the best way to deal with Robby and Red would be to take the battery out of the Garmin chirp and replace it with a different Garmin chirp—one that *they* had programmed.

That was the only way they felt they could change the target, because once a chirp is programmed, no other Garmin device can alter the programming.

The thieves placed their chirp device exactly where the old one was, and they called it by the same name.

They did change the coordinates for the cache it pointed to, however. They provided instructions that looked very much like the old instructions, but the coordinates pointed to a location nearly one hundred yards from the one Mr. Gordon had intended his son to find.

The new target was an abandoned nineteenth-century exploratory vertical mineshaft. It had been dug by Finnish miners in 1893. As was the case with most of the Upper Peninsula vertical shafts, it was not truly vertical—at least not past the twenty-foot initial vertical drop. It continued to descend at that point, but on an incline of about thirty-five degrees for the first one hundred and fifty feet. Once past the incline, the mining company had dug a few horizontal drifts.

However, even though they had reason to hope for success, one of their horizontal drifts passed too close to a particularly vibrant spring. Initially, the inflow was barely more than seepage. But little by little it increased in volume.

When it finally broke through it was like a small stream—so much water began filling the drifts the miners could not keep up with it. They were forced to give up on the mine when the water level reached the bottom of the incline.

Mining regulations were lax regarding the closing of a mine during that period. They simply covered the ten-foot opening with three-inch rough-cut oak planks, with a second layer of similar planks placed on top of the first but running perpendicular.

On top of the wood roof, they placed two layers of heavy tarpaper.

Tarpaper at that time was a relatively recent invention. While originally the product was constructed by pouring hot tar onto paper, by the 1880s the process had evolved to using materials other than paper, such as asbestos. Later, once research emerged regarding the potential health hazards involved with asbestos, other materials such as fiberglass and polyester replaced asbestos as the bonding agent.

Interestingly, the earliest popular application for the use of tarpaper to waterproof roofs occurred during the California Gold Rush. Prospectors would construct rough wooden structures at the site of their claims, live in them for a short time, and then move on. Tarpaper was cheap and easy to use. And when they were no longer needed, the little tarpaper prospector shanties could be abandoned without regrets.

At the time the Finnish miners were closing this mine, the only tarpaper available to them was asbestos laced, so that is what they used. Once the planks were securely in place, they then spread out a little topsoil over the tarpaper and posted a warning sign.

With that, the mine was considered temporarily closed. Permanent closure would have required trucking in massive amounts of fill. Such an effort would cost more than the fledgling mining company could afford.

So, instead of moving in that direction, the principal parties decided to dissolve the company and join forces with another, more established enterprise successfully operating to the west, in the Marquette Gold District.

Amazingly, the tarpaper-covered lumber used to cover the vertical shaft held up well. In fact, the thieves would not have known about the mine's existence had they not stumbled upon it while doing research at the Mining University in Houghton.

The records on file did not provide coordinates; however, they were sufficiently detailed so that the thieves were able to locate the general area.

And then, with the aid of a shovel and pickax, they were actually able to find the lightly buried boards. Because the mine had been dug on the crest of a small hill, and because high-quality roofing material was used to waterproof its opening, the mine remained virtually intact just as it was when the Finns left it.

As soon as they had determined the exact middle of the shaft, they took a reading for coordinates: 46.351928,-86.839108. They programmed those numbers into the Garmin chirp, which they had substituted for the unit programmed by Titus Gordon.

Then the thieves carefully scraped off the top layer of soil and leaves. Next they removed the entire top layer of oak timbers and the tarpaper. Those they loaded onto two John Deere M-Gator A3 ATVs and hauled them over to a large patch of very thick brush to hide them temporarily.

Their intention was to return later and restore the mine's opening to its previous state.

After storing the timbers, they then used a battery-powered handsaw to cut all of the boards nearly through in three places, rendering them unable to support over one hundred pounds of weight. They started with the middle cut, then made the other two cuts using the edge of the mine's opening to support their weight.

Once finished with the saw, they used a portable vacuum cleaner to pick up all the sawdust.

After they had finished cleaning up all the evidence, they

spread out a light covering of soil and covered that with leaves and sprinklings of twigs and branches.

Once two days and nights had passed, the site of the trap did not reveal the danger that lurked beneath the surface.

The morning dews, the gentle forest breezes, and even the constant foraging of squirrels, foxes, and fowls of every indigenous variety, soon evened out the terrain, rendering the very existence of the cavernous trap beneath the surface virtually invisible to even the studied human eye.

The trap was set. All that it required was the weight of two teenage boys and, probably, a dog.

Chapter 49
The boys ditch their bikes

Once they reached the point where Addis Lake Road branched left off USFS 2482, Robby said, "Now we start looking for a good place to lock up our bikes. In another mile and a half or so, we're going to have to start going on foot."

That sounded good to Red. While it was not in his nature to complain, his feet, particularly his left foot, did not agree with pedaling a bike. Less than five years earlier, he had severely injured his left foot in an effort to escape from foster care.

He had found himself placed with Lawrence and Milly Klyburn, a family who lived near Trout Lake. Chippewa County Child Services had chosen that particular foster home because it was located in the far northwest corner of the county. Red had a history of running away from other placements, and authorities thought that if they sent him all the way out there, he would be content to remain, at least for a while.

But Red was not satisfied.

On the drive from the Soo, he had spotted the Canadian National 9473 running north out of Trout Lake. He determined immediately that would be his ticket back home. *After all,* he thought, *where else could it be going?* And from the Soo he would hop on the Sugar Island Ferry.

Red remained at the Klyburn home only long enough for the caseworker to drink a cup of coffee with the house parents. As soon as they turned their backs, Red took off by jumping out of a second-story bedroom window.

He headed straight for the railroad track and began running along it to the northeast. When he reached the Trout Lake train station, he spotted a pile of shipping pallets and hid out there behind it until he saw the Canadian Northern begin to pull out. Checking to be sure he had not been spotted, he darted between two cars of the moving train and tucked himself up into the underbelly of one. He then maneuvered his body until he found a reasonably comfortable position.

Even though it was only late November, the daytime temperatures still hovered in the mid-twenties. While Red somehow managed to keep from succumbing to hypothermia, he unfortunately did not emerge unscathed. In an effort to keep his feet from freezing, he alternately rested one foot and then the other on the axle of the train, hoping that the friction generated by the spinning axle would warm his foot.

However, eventually the cold conquered his efforts. As his left foot grew numb, the constant motion of the axle ate through his shoe and literally wore off much of his left foot.

When the train arrived in the Soo, he jumped off and tried to walk. But by then both feet were frostbitten—two of his toes were totally exposed and dangled out of the side of his left shoe.

Amazingly, Red healed up pretty well. Doctors managed to save both of his feet, less one toe on his left foot. After time and therapy, he regained strength and the use of both feet.

Still, as was the case on this day, certain activities irritated his feet, particularly his more severely damaged left foot.

Red would be happy to lock up the bike and walk for a while.

"Check this out," Robby said as he slammed on his brakes. "This looks like the *perfect* place."

Robby had spotted a very heavy-duty gate about fifty yards off the road. It had been installed to prevent any type of motorized traffic from traveling down an old logging trail. The sign on it read: "Foot Traffic Only."

So the boys jumped off their bikes and pushed them down the old trail. When they reached the gate, they picked them up and placed each of them flat alongside one of the supporting posts and secured them to the thick steel using their heavy-duty bike locks.

"Just for kicks," Robby said, "I'm gonna get a GPS reading on this location. It'd be easy to get turned around and forget how to get back to our bikes."

He logged the coordinates into his cell phone as a "contact," and then they got back on USFS 2482 and continued south toward the designated point of departure. Before they had left Sugar Island, Robby had already determined that the best way for him to find the rock formation would be to retrace the route he and his father had taken.

While Titus and Robby had approached not using bikes at all, they did hike down USFS 2482—precisely the same route as Robby and Red were using.

Both Red and Buddy were glad to be hiking instead of riding—Red because his feet were tired, and Buddy because hiking meant he was able to move slower and rest more frequently.

After they had traveled about a mile more down the road, Robby said, "Somewhere not too far ahead, this road will veer a little off to the left. Just before it does, we're going to head directly west.

"That should put us right by a small lake," Robby said. "It's really little more than a pond. On the map, it's called *Line Lake*. But Dad always called it *Lime Lake*. He figured the maps misspelled the name of the lake since it wasn't a popular tourist attraction or anything. So I think I'll just call it Lime Lake, too."

The coolness of the forest made the boys eager to keep moving. The trees protected them from the summer sun, and the excitement about the close proximity to their destination amplified their impatience to get there.

"Once we reach the lake we should head about three hundred and fifty yards directly west of the north end of the pond. We can pace that off. And then we turn directly north."

Red then texted so Robby could read it, "Thts whre beepr is?"

"Right," Robby said. "If we stay heading straight north, in about another three hundred yards we should begin to pick up the signal from the chirp."

The two thieves had taken a position several hundred feet west and south of the mineshaft. From that location, they could hide in the brush yet still have a clear view of the approach they anticipated the boys would take.

Their plan was a good one. They would lie in wait for Robby and Red to detect the chirp they had placed where the old one had been. But instead of locating it close to the ground, as Titus Gordon had, they positioned theirs in the branches of a tree right next to the original placement.

They knew that the signal from the chirp would reach farther if it were elevated. And they wanted to do everything they possibly could to ensure the boys would detect its signal.

Once the boys received the coordinates the thieves had programmed into the chirp, they thought that they would hurry over to the trap they had prepared for them.

And that is exactly how it played out.

Robby and Red reached the point on USFS 2482 where it turned slightly to the east. So they left the road and began hiking directly west.

Chapter 50
Line Lake Swamp

Soon they came upon the Line Lake swamp.

"This is it!" Robby exclaimed. "This is the lake my dad called *Lime* Lake. We're getting close now!"

The two boys skirted to the north of the lake and began taking long steps and counting them.

"This should be about right," Robby said, clearly excited. "Now we turn north."

He took a look at his Garmin Montana to be sure it was working, and he began walking north.

"We don't really have to count anymore," he said. "The GPS will tell us when we get close to the chirp."

After about three hundred yards he got a signal.

Looking down at his GPS, he read, "Head northwest one hundred yards to 46.351928,-86.839108."

Robby excitedly showed the display to Red. Pointing toward a small clearing to the northwest, he said, "See that little mound? That's about a hundred yards to the northwest. Let's head toward it."

As they approached the trap, Robby said, "I don't recall this being located on a hill. But it was getting dark when I was here before. Anyway, we should be *almost* there."

The two thieves adjusted their binoculars.

"I think they are about to take a bath in very dirty water," the man chuckled.

Robby checked the coordinates to determine they had found the right spot. "This must be it."

First Robby stepped out onto the half-sawn planks. And then Red did as well. Finally, Buddy joined them.

"This sounds hollow," Robby said, stomping his right foot and hearing an echo.

At that very second the female thief let out a muted shout, "Yes! It worked!"

The planks had given way as planned, and all three of them—Robby, Red, and Buddy—dropped into the mineshaft just as though the trapdoor lever had been pulled on their gallows.

Chapter 51

Like nothing they could have imagined

It was not as though all the boards gave way at once. Initially, the only board that failed was the one Robby tapped with his foot to hear the echo. But its splitting started a chain reaction.

Initially, Robby fell straight down through the opening created by the vacating plank. But his backpack struck the plank behind him, thrusting him forward and momentarily retarding his descent.

Robby's first reaction was to reach out to his friend, which he did. He shot his hand forward as he started to fall. Red grabbed for it but missed.

Robby's hand slid down Red's pants, his fingers finally catching in the top of Red's right shoe. That momentarily slowed his descent, but it did not save him from falling. The shock of the extra weight exerted on Red's foot by Robby trying to stop his fall snapped the board Red was standing on, drawing him toward the abyss as well.

It happened so quickly the boys could not escape the pit.

Buddy reacted by sinking his teeth into Red's backpack, and he was pulled into the hole with the boys.

The thieves could not have hoped for a better result. In fact, they believed that if even one of the boys or the dog were to have fallen into the mine they could still make their plan work. Were that to have been the case, the thieves planned to go to the scene and offer assistance. However, instead of helping, they would have clubbed the boys with shovels and dumped them into the mineshaft.

Once all three victims had been disposed of, the thieves would break out the remaining half-sawn boards and throw them into the mineshaft. Afterward, they would retrieve the intact boards that they had stashed away on the two ATVs and reconstruct the mineshaft's roof.

And with both boys and the dog inside the hole, that's exactly what they began to do.

But because they had seen all three of their victims tumble into the mine without any intervention on their part, they had no reason to inspect the mineshaft. Instead, they headed directly over to pick up the ATVs and the planks they had removed earlier.

It took them twenty minutes to knock out the half-sawn boards and replace them with the intact boards. They then covered the planks with new tarpaper and finished off the project by shoveling loose topsoil onto the makeshift roof.

After they had spread out leaves and brush, it had virtually the same appearance it did when the boys initially ventured out upon it. It looked like it had for the past one hundred years.

Once finished, the thieves did not say a single word to each other. They simply exchanged smiles, mounted their Gators, and activated their tracking devices to locate the boys' bikes.

"Shit," she said. "They've locked them up. And you didn't think to bring bolt cutters. Right?"

He didn't respond as he stripped off the tracking transmitters.

"Can't do anything about these bikes," he said, "but without these transmitters nothing can be traced back to us."

Again they did not say a word as they jumped on their Gators and headed back to the campground. There they loaded the ATVs on the large trailer that was still connected to the rear of their motorhome, and within minutes they had checked out.

* * *

The situation for the two boys and Buddy seemed impossible.

When they landed, which was about fifteen feet below the surface, all three of them slid down the thirty-degree incline until they hit water. All but Buddy momentarily disappeared beneath the surface. Sliding backward down the incline, he fought the incline so vehemently that by the time he reached the water he had broken his momentum to the point that he was not swallowed up by the stagnant sludge as the two boys were.

Red came to the surface almost immediately. At first he tried to adjust his eyes to the darkness but soon realized it was no use. He called out to Robby with an utterance that sounded more animal than human, but Robby did not respond.

As best he could, he continued barking noises in order to elicit some sort of reaction from Robby. When none followed, he locked his fingers into the thick mud and extended his legs downward into the mud. He recalled that Robby had dropped a few feet to his left, so he slid over and searched the mud there. Still he had no luck.

After his fifth effort, his foot struck something soft, and it moved. It was Robby. *Why doesn't he grab onto my leg?* Red wondered.

Red freed one hand and dropped down into the mud. He felt around with his free hand until he located Robby's hair. He grabbed a handful and pulled his friend to the surface.

The small amount of light that pierced the opening proved useless even for Red's fully-dilated pupils. He had to examine Robby for injury by running his fingers over his friend's body. Robby still had not moved.

Chapter 52

It looked bleak

Red could barely get enough traction on the muddy incline to pull himself partially out of the water. It was all he could do to keep Robby's face above the surface.

When the two thieves began ripping out the half-sawn boards, it allowed more light to shine into the mine. Red made all the noise he could to summon help, not realizing that the two people above him had no interest in saving their lives.

Red felt Robby's neck and found a strong pulse. He knew that was a good sign. But when he felt around on Robby's head, he quickly discovered the cause of his friend's unconsciousness. There, on the back of his skull, was a goose egg half the size of a golf ball. As Red ran his fingers over the bump, he could feel a large, warm open wound. At first he could not determine whether what he was feeling was mud or blood. But as the hot sticky ooze ran across his hand, he assumed that the moisture he felt was blood. It was clear to Red that Robby had a bad concussion and a severe open wound.

As the two thieves removed the initial layer of planks above, they simply discarded them by dropping them into the mine. When they struck the surface of the incline, they slid the fifty feet down the slippery incline just as the boys and Buddy had done fifteen minutes before.

Buddy was quick enough to avoid being struck, but Red was not so fortunate.

After the first two sixty-pound planks bounced off him, he pulled Robby by the hair to the side of the mine and hung onto a rock that was protruding. He turned his back as best he could toward the oncoming threat.

Fortunately, only the first two struck Red—and neither of them at a speed sufficient to injure.

After finding futile his efforts to summon aid from the two people who were working above them, Red finally gave up that effort. He rightly concluded that he, Robby, and Buddy had walked into a trap.

So, he silently turned his attention to his friend, who was beginning to stir.

"What happened?" Robby asked. "Where are we?"

While he would have liked to explain to Robby what had happened, all Red could do was comfort his friend. And, at least for the moment, Red had no plan of escape.

"We fell in a hole," Robby figured out. "Is that where we are? In a hole?"

Red placed Robby's hand on his head and nodded.

"Is there an opening?"

Red nodded.

"But we can't get to it, can we?"

Red shook his head.

"My head is killing me. I must have bumped it."

Red nodded and then guided Robby's hand so that he could feel the deep gash.

"Wow. I did that when I fell?"

Red nodded. Robby could not see his signal but recognized his silence as agreement.

Just then Robby heard the two people working above.

"Hey!" Robby yelled. "There's people up there. Help! Help us! We're down here. Can you hear me? Help!"

After a few short moments, Robby yelled again, "Help!"

"What's up with them?" Robby finally asked Red. "They must be able to hear me."

Red's failure to respond told Robby that the people above were never going to help them. But Robby was not willing to accept that as fact.

This time Robby felt around until he located Red's head and dug the fingers of his right hand into Red's mud-matted hair. Red slowly nodded his head.

Even though at one point the thieves had removed all the planks at the mouth of the mineshaft, the light that shone down did not strike anything but the black floor of the mine, so virtually none of it reached the boys.

Robby then realized what was happening. While the concussion blocked his memory of precisely how they had arrived at their current positions, the fact that there were people above who were not interested in helping them led Robby to the correct conclusion.

"They want us to die, don't they?" Robby asked. "They threw us down here. And they *want* us to die. Is that it?"

Chapter 53

Searching for a way out

Red nodded.

"Here," Robby said, untangling his fingers from Red's hair. "I think we can let go of each other. I think I can keep myself up."

When Red let loose of his friend, Robby, not able to get traction on the muddy incline, started sliding down deeper into the mud.

Red quickly grabbed him and pulled him back up.

"How're you able to keep from sliding?" Robby asked.

Red took Robby's right hand, guided it to the wall, and helped him feel around for something to grab onto.

Robby wrapped his fingers around the edge of a vertical oak timber used by the miners to help support the roof.

"*That* helps," he said.

Robby took a few moments to think about their situation, and then he said, "I hear Buddy. He must be okay. Right?"

Red did not reply, knowing that his silence would be interpreted as a positive nonresponse.

"This is not a hole. Right? This is a *mine*. The floor is at an angle. Is that right?"

Again Red was silent.

"Do you think Buddy could make it up the incline?"

Red grunted.

"No? It must be very slippery. Right?"

Red nodded his head but remained silent.

While Robby could not see Red nodding, he correctly interpreted Red's lack of response.

"We've got to find a way outta here before hypothermia sets in. At least to get out of the water. We don't have long."

Red again took Robby's cold hand, placed it on his own head, and nodded.

"You've got a plan?" Robby asked hopefully.

This time Red grunted in a telling fashion.

"Neither do I," Robby finally said.

Buddy breathed a mournful whine, followed by another.

After a long period of silence, Robby began to cry. Ever since his parents had been killed he did that a lot—cry. But up until now he'd never broken down in front of other people. Now he didn't care.

While Red could not see his friend, he knew Robby was crying.

Red doubled his determination to find a way to safety.

Chapter 54

Delta 3740

The flight I would recommend is Delta's 3740—that's the one I use when I come to the resort. It departs at 9:05 a.m. from LaGuardia and arrives at 1:35 in the afternoon. One stop. I emailed her the info. Should I contact her again to be sure she's followed up on it?"

"She said she was good with our making the arrangements," Jack said. "But she's going to have to book the flight herself. I think you should give her a day and then call her."

"I told her that we had to pick the boys up in Munising later this evening, so it would be best if she could make the trip Friday or later. I said she would be welcome to stay for as long as she wished, but that she should plan on at least three full days, unless she has critical business pending."

Kate was used to conducting interrogations. She knew that the person being questioned always has a speech memorized and that, if the interrogator wants to get to the real truth, it's best to return to the issue several times. Allow the suspect to deliver the speech, perhaps more than once, and then go for blood.

This would be particularly true in this case, because Pam would most likely be meeting with the sheriff as well. That would be the best opportunity to deliver her canned speech. And then Jack and Kate would spend the remainder of the time getting to the real story. Jack would cook up something extraordinary, such as his whitefish specialty, and they would serve her a glass or two of a nice white wine from the resort's wine cellar, and that should hopefully carry Pam well past her canned speech.

"That's right!" Jack said. "We have to pick the boys up tonight. That had totally slipped my mind. I guess they don't want to exercise the extra-day option."

"Well, aren't you a fine grandpa?" Kate quipped.

"I'm the *uncle*. Let's get that straight," he responded. "*You're* going to have to get busy if I'm ever going to be a grandpa."

Kate did not respond to his words. That was an *old news* comment that she did not wish to acknowledge, much less revisit.

"I figure we leave here at two," she said. "And we can go straight to the casino in Christmas—that's a town just west of Munising. I've heard that their soups are really good. A friend told me she got a bowl of split-pea and it was out of this world."

Jack thought about it for a moment, and then chuckled, "I think that comment qualifies as an oxymoron."

"What?"

"Juxtaposing 'pea soup' and 'out of this world,'" he said.

"You say that only because you've not had a bowl of really good split-pea soup," Kate countered. "The next time you visit me in New York, I'll take you to my deli. I *promise* you'll like it."

"Why don't you just cook some up here?" Jack said, trying to corner her. "I'm sure the boys would love it. Make a list of ingredients and I'll pick them up for you."

"First of all," she retorted, "you know I don't like to cook. And second, you're just bearing out what I said about you—*bad grandpa.*"

Jack laughed, and then he said, "I'm a little surprised we haven't heard from them—the boys, that is. They must be having a great time."

Chapter 55

This ain't no swimmin' pool

The pair of thieves at the top developed a system of removing and disposing of the planks.

First they lifted one end and pulled it toward them until it cleared the far edge. As it started to fall, they would give it a bit of a shove. In almost every case, the plank struck the far wall with sufficient force to break it at the center cut.

Those that did not break would become lodged diagonally against the far wall, and when the next plank was launched, it would snap those intact boards that remained leaning.

While most of the boards immediately slid down the slick incline, some piled up on the steeply slanted floor, forming a stack four-or-more-planks thick.

Eventually, even the laggards succumbed to gravity and, with the aid of spring-fed slime, shot down the incline like an armada of speedboats.

Red and Robby did all they could do to brace themselves for the onslaughts. They could hear the attacks coming. First they heard the boards striking the floor, followed by the sounds of them banging against the walls.

Finally, the torpedoes struck their targets—the boys at the bottom. Single planks were not difficult to guard against. Red had captured one of the boards and handed one end to Robby. As the planks neared them, they held the board out in front of them to absorb the impact.

But when a whole stack slid together, it would strike with sufficient force to knock them back into the deeper water.

And that's when it happened. They knew that a substantial pile of planks was building up. They could hear the boards crashing and breaking above, but nothing was sliding toward them.

Eventually, the pile gave way and began to slide. They heard it crashing against the walls on its voyage toward them.

But just before it struck them, it stopped. At first they could not determine what had happened. The noise just stopped—apparently right in front of them.

Red waited until silence indicated that their captors had finished working above them. And then, reaching up as far as he could, Red felt around on the incline. Finally, he grunted his excitement. Robby did not understand what stimulated his friend's elation, but he suspected something good was about to happen.

What Red had discovered was that about five feet up the incline two boards had become firmly lodged across the incline, and they were holding back the descent of more than a dozen other boards above them.

Upon further examination, Red determined how they were able to do it.

Chapter 56

A plan is brewing

Red discovered that, as these particular boards slid downward, one end of each struck the opposite wall of the incline. And at precisely the same time, the other ends of the boards met in the middle to form an inverted "V." The force of the boards sliding downward caused the first two boards to dig firmly into each other in the middle of the incline.

As soon as Red determined exactly what had happened, he immediately saw the potential of what he had found.

Using his fortuitous board-dam discovery, Red pulled himself out of the muck and up onto the incline and then crawled on top of the pile of boards.

After he had flattened out an area large enough for a staging, he then reached down and helped Robby up as well.

"How does this work?" a grateful Robby said as he began to feel around to figure out how Red had been able to pull him upward.

Robby reached up and found where the two boards came together and pulled himself completely up and out of the mud. Turning around and sitting down on the boards, he stuck his right leg down and called for Buddy.

At first the dog just whined. But then Robby felt Buddy's nose on his leg.

"Come on up, Buddy. Come on. Get up here. You can do it."

Buddy made an effort to jump, but he could not generate enough leverage in the mud to launch himself up.

So Robby allowed his whole body to slide back down into the mud, all the way to where Buddy was stranded.

Buddy was not exactly standing. His front paws were dug into the mud on the floor, but just below the water level. His hindquarters were basically floating, and occasionally he would propel himself forward slightly by kicking against the muddy water with his hind legs.

When Robby dropped into the water beside him, Buddy wasted no time. The dog knew immediately what to do. He dug his claws into Robby's pants and pulled himself out of the water, and he finally pulled himself to safety by virtually walking up Robby's back.

And then, just as they expected, Buddy managed the most energetic shake that could be imagined. Both boys turned their faces away from the dog until he had finished.

Discovery of the board-dam allowed all three of them to escape the heat-sucking mud. For nearly half an hour they rested.

Their clothes were wet, muddy, and covered with slime; it was in their hair and on their faces. When they had slid down the incline, their backpacks, which they were wearing at the time they'd fallen, had momentarily disappeared with them beneath the surface of the mud.

But for right now, they were out of the mud and beginning to dry off. Even though it was a small victory, all three recognized that it was a victory nonetheless.

It was at that point Red had another idea. But because he had no way to explain it to Robby, he just set about implementing it.

Whatever the power behind the provision of physical materials—whether it was luck, fate, or perhaps even divine intervention—the plan that emerged was solely the result of Red's ingenuity.

Even though Robby could not see the progress Red was making, he was aware that Red was removing all the boards that had built up ahead of them on the board-dam.

So Robby took his cue from that and slid back down into the muddy water and began handing up the boards that were floating below. He would slide one up the incline, and as Red could find the boards, he would receive and pile them above a second board-dam, which he had already constructed.

Once he became aware that he needed help, Robby coaxed Buddy back into the mud.

"Fetch," he commanded. And Buddy obeyed. Swimming out to where the mud met the sloping roof, Buddy recovered all the boards that were afloat and brought them to Robby.

"That's it," Robby said after he and Buddy had retrieved and passed up more than a dozen boards out of the mud. "At least that's all we can find."

Red grunted his approval as he helped Robby and Buddy to get out of the mud for the second time.

Again, Buddy took the opportunity to launch chunks of mud and debris all over the two boys—they both had another good laugh.

Robby, however, was not as energetic as he had been. He admitted he was tired and needed to rest.

"I'm beginning to lose the feeling in my arms and legs," he confessed. "If it's okay, I'd just like to dry off and maybe rest up a little."

Chapter 57

Buddy knew

Buddy sensed Robby's problem, and he carefully made his way over to where the boy was sitting and nuzzled in close beside him to help him get warmed up.

Red had no problem with Robby's request. He realized that his friend had been seriously injured when he fell. And besides, Red really didn't need help at this stage. Years of living on his own in the Sugar Island wilderness had not only toughened Red, but it also galvanized his resourcefulness and resolve.

Red then pulled himself up to the second board-dam, and from that position he created a third inverted V and then restacked all the planks ahead of that board-dam.

Fortunately, the grooves that were sawn into the boards did not minimize their effectiveness in this application. Because no pressure was being applied opposite the saw marks, they did not affect the integrity of Red's project.

In each case, Red would first lift a new plank from the pile and shove one end hard against the left wall about even with the top of the board-dam from which he was working. He would then place the other end of the board about six feet above the centermost part of the existing board-dam. To hold it in place, he would temporarily lay one of the unused boards on top of its apex while he positioned the right board.

He would then lock them together in the middle, tugging on the new inverted V to be sure it would adequately support weight. When satisfied that his construction would be strong, he would move on up.

It was going well. The soft sticky mud on the sloped floor seemed almost to reach up and grab the boards from Red's hands. And once in place, the vacuum created around them by the mud locked them tight.

And so his work progressed, until he reached the area directly beneath the roof that the two thieves had by then completed.

Red then turned around and headed back down to where he'd left Robby and Buddy. When he reached the lowest board-dam, he made a noise in hopes of eliciting a response from his friend.

Robby did not respond, but Buddy did whine softly.

Red felt his way over to where he had left Robby and Buddy. Red gently shook Robby's shoulder and accompanied his touch with an audible.

When his friend didn't move, he repeated his efforts. After he tried to arouse Robby a third time, Red realized that Robby had lost consciousness.

Red then pulled Robby up the incline a little farther, making sure that he was securely positioned on the upside of the first inverted V and not in any danger of slipping into the mud.

Red then petted Buddy on the back and uttered a special sound, which Buddy had learned to mean "stay."

Buddy understood that Red's friend was in trouble and that Red had just instructed him to take care of Robby.

Buddy, who was already lying next to Robby, sniffed around until he found the open wound on Robby's head and began licking it. And then Buddy drew his warmth in even more closely to Robby's still body. It was as though Buddy understood exactly the task Red had given him that he should keep Robby warm.

Red realized that the lives of all three of them, especially Robby's, depended on his not giving up.

With renewed energy, Red bolted back toward the top of the incline. At first he did not realize just how close he was to the top. But when his outstretched arm hit some strange unexpected objects, he realized that he had reached the top of the incline.

Chapter 58

View from the top

He looked up and saw a tiny dot of light. *That's the roof,* he correctly reasoned. *That's where we fell through.*

For a few moments he just lay there on the floor thinking. *This was no accident. This was a trap. Whoever replaced those boards intended that we should die in here. But why?*

The floor at that point was made slick by constant seepage

from a spring and from the drainage of decaying surface vegetation. But as Red felt his way around, he discovered a number of smaller boards and other pieces of debris stuck in the mud, particularly farther up the incline.

In fact, Red found that when he crawled past the point that was directly beneath the roof, the floor of the incline seemed to level out. He even found that he could stand, at least as long as he dug his lower foot into the mud. He felt around and grabbed hold of a firm object in what appeared to be a collection of refuse piled at the topmost point of the incline.

Red fingered around on the debris until he discovered a flat place where he could sit down. He needed to rest.

The wooden roof was directly above and slightly down the slope from where he was sitting. He couldn't get an accurate determination of the height of the roof above him, but there was a small shaft of light needling through the tarpaper, all the way to the floor. His eyes followed it from floor to roof several times.

I'm guessing a little under twenty feet, he reasoned. *No way I can reach it.*

Red sat there still and silent for several minutes, as though waiting for Jack and Kate to start removing the boards above.

After a while Red carefully made his way back down to the tiny beam of light. Holding out his hand until the light struck it, he then followed it to the floor. There, using a pointed sliver of metal he had found on the floor, he drew a cross in the mud directly through the point where the light illuminated the floor.

And then he went back to his seat to think. *I've made it this far,* he thought, *but I don't see how we get outta here. That's twenty feet—straight up.*

Red had no idea how long they would be stuck in the mine. Gauging the angle and direction of the beam of light, he determined that it was about two p.m.

After what he estimated to be an hour, he made another cross.

Three o'clock, he reasoned.

When he bent down to place the four p.m. marking, the marker he held in his hand touched something he had not expected.

Chapter 59
They will find the bodies next year

May I see your license, registration, and proof of insurance, please?" Officer Stephen Randall of the Michigan State Police requested. He had just pulled Glenda and Jeremy over on M-28 six miles west of Shelter Bay.

Jeremy, wearing his camo with a Toronto baseball cap, found the registration and proof of insurance in an envelope stowed in the center console. He removed his driver's license from his wallet and handed the three items to the officer.

Once the officer left, the attack began.

"How many times did I tell you to slow down?" Glenda said angrily. She was hungry, tired, and just wanted to find a hot shower and a beer.

"I *knew* something like this was going to happen."

"Just relax, babe," he said in a calming voice as he lit up a cigarette. "I wasn't speeding. I'm not drunk. We've both got our seatbelts on. And my name is not Willie Nelson. This is probably just some routine fact-finding mission. We'll be fine."

"They don't just pull people over for no good reason," Glenda fired back, her dark brown eyes glaring. "You must have been doing *something* wrong."

"Well, I'm sure we'll soon find out," Jeremy said, sneaking a glance into his rearview mirror and spotting the officer walking toward him.

But Officer Randall did not return directly to the front of the motorhome. Instead, he stopped between the motorhome and the trailer and remained there for a couple minutes.

"What could he be doing?" Jeremy muttered. "Maybe one of my chains came off."

Finally, the officer came up to talk to Jeremy.

"Mr. Manson, are you the owner of this motorhome?"

"It's a rental. It's under Glenda's name."

"And how about this trailer. Do you own it?"

"Yes," Jeremy replied. "Is there something wrong with it?"

"Do you know how long this motorhome is?"

"According to the paperwork, it's a forty-five footer."

"And how long is the trailer?"

"It's twenty feet long," Jeremy said.

"Do you know about the Michigan Lemon Law Road Laws?"

"I'm not sure I know what you mean," Jeremy replied. "I thought I read that the total legal length allowed was sixty-five feet. Forty-five plus twenty. That should be sixty-five."

"Right," the officer said. "But you're not counting the tongue. The manufacturers of enclosed trailers like that do not include the tongue in the way they list length.

"That would make the total combined length more like sixty-seven or sixty-eight feet. And that is clearly not permitted by Michigan law."

"Oh shit!" Jeremy exclaimed. "You're right. I should have thought of that."

Glenda turned her face toward the windshield, rolled her eyes, and sighed in deep disgust.

"Officer, I'm so sorry," Jeremy apologized. "I generally pull the trailer with my pickup. It was just my carelessness. I should have measured it before setting out."

"Your license says you're from Houghton. Is that where you are headed?" the officer asked.

"Yes," Jeremy said. "I teach there."

The officer continued writing his citation, and then he handed it to Jeremy. "I could cite you for this violation, make you find someplace over here on North Point Road to park it, and then return for it with a shorter vehicle. You know that, right?"

"I know that."

"I'm writing you up a warning this time," the officer said, with a smile. "If you'd made me get out my tape measure, it might have been a different story."

"Thanks, officer," Jeremy said. "I won't do this again."

"Have a nice day," the officer said to Jeremy. "And you, ma'am," he said, looking past Jeremy. "You have a nice day too."

The officer had observed Glenda's various shades of grimace and wanted to ease her frustration.

Glenda did not look at him, but she did manage a grumpy, "Thank you."

Once the officer left, she began complaining.

"This is just grand. Just super," she said. "Now they've got a record of our having been in the area. They record these things, you know. I knew you would find some way to screw this up. I should have asked Art to help me with this part. He *never* messes things up like you do."

Jeremy did not respond. He knew she was venting. That was her nature. Whenever faced with a negative situation, that was how she always reacted.

But he also knew that she would quickly get over it. He loved her, and he believed she loved him too. And, he was deathly afraid of Art.

"I'm going to give Art a call and see what he thinks about all this," Glenda said, looking for her phone.

After a frustrating few minutes of searching through her things, Glenda belted out at Jeremy, "Do you have my phone? I can't find my damn phone! Have you seen it?"

Chapter 60
The sheriff wants in

"I can't believe the sheriff," Kate said to her father after disconnecting from a phone call. "He's already calling back to see if we've got a solid date and time for him to meet with Pam. He must have nothing better to do."

"This has potential for a problem," Jack responded. "I need to meet with her first, alone. Before she talks to the sheriff. We need to make some decisions—Pam, Roger, and I. We might have to slide that meeting with the sheriff back a bit. If not indefinitely."

"How would we do that if we've already promised the sheriff he could sit in and ask questions?" Kate asked.

"When we go to pick up the boys," Jack said, "we'll rattle that around a bit. I would like to get Roger's input. After all, he is right at the center of this. It really wouldn't surprise me if Allison had information that Pam doesn't have. I'd even bet that she knows …"

Jack caught himself and stopped in the middle of his sentence.

"Do you think you're going to share with me some of what you know before Pam gets here?"

"Right now, this is what I'm thinking," Jack replied as he pulled up a chair in Kate's office.

"I will have you with me when I pick up Pam at the airport. We will then find a good spot to talk, perhaps at that coffee shop we like in the Soo—it used to be called Joey's …"

"Yeah," Kate interrupted. "The place Sheriff Green was talking about. After Joey's death, the new owner renamed it. I think it's now called Caffeine … Caffeine *Something*."

"We could get a booth, and the three of us could discuss the matter. Find out exactly what Pam knows. I'd like to get Roger on the phone at the same time. Maybe even bring in that other party. I'll see what Roger has to say about it. I think I'll give him a call on our way over to pick up the boys. You then can listen to one end of the conversation and learn what you need to learn, but without my actually stating it to you as fact."

Chapter 61
The flashlight

This is a cell phone!" Red mumbled as he picked it up and fingered the "home" button. "No service, but at least now I've got a flashlight."

He turned it on and shined it down the incline to check on Robby. He confirmed that his friend had not moved and that Buddy was lying next to him to keep him warm. Buddy was extremely smart, even for a recently feathered-out golden retriever. Red had trusted him with his life, and now his friend's life.

Red then used the light to survey his surroundings. Just as he had suspected, he confirmed that the floor began to level out just past the point directly beneath where the wooden roof ended. When the mineworkers had closed the project down, they'd backfilled the shaft with all sorts of debris. Much of it had slid down the incline and into the water. But trash that landed on the flat part of the floor stuck. And so a large amount of the discard had built into a pile right up to the point where the floor began to slope downward.

They knew that they would have had a very difficult time filling the whole mine back up, so for the area above the incline—but before the point where the rock was substantial enough to support the earth above—they constructed the wooden roof.

Red made his way to the backfill that had been dumped into the mine to see if he could find something useful. He saw a wooden ladder that the early workers must have used in the mine, but it crumbled in his hands when he tried to lift it.

In the middle of the floor, but covered with dirt and debris, he discovered a rail car. *Must be rails under this mud*, he reasoned. So he looked around and found an iron rod half exposed in the rubble.

Constructed by a blacksmith from a four-foot piece of five-eighths-inch hot-rolled steel, it had a looped handle at one end and a right-angle pointed hook on the other. Red used it to dig around where he suspected the rails must be.

Even if I find a rail, I wonder if I'll even be able to lift it off the floor?

He soon discovered that at least the first twenty feet of the rails had been removed when the mine was closed.

Why would they waste time and energy removing the rails and then leave the ore car? he asked himself.

Using his light and steel poker, he began prodding through the junk, searching around for anything else that he might use to lift himself to the wooden roof.

He noticed that the mud was mounded up higher on the floor at the left wall than on the right.

After he had dug some of the mud away, he poked the end of the rod into the mound and heard a slight metallic sound.

I'll bet that's where they discarded the rails they had pulled up, he thought. M*aybe just the damaged ones.*

He was right. There were six ten-foot mine rails buried under the mud. They were stuck together by one hundred years of oxidation.

He checked his battery. *Eighty-five percent*, he read. So he propped the cell phone up and used its light.

Every forty-five seconds the cell would go to standby and turn dark. But that was perfect. He would chip away at the rails in the light, and when it shut down he would keep working in the dark for as long as he could. He would return to the cell every few minutes and re-activate the light.

Eventually, he was able to pry one rail out of the clump of oxidation. At first he managed to lift the end of the rail only an inch or two. But finally, by using both hands and a board, he muscled it high enough to wrench it off the pile and toward the center of the mine. He then dropped it hard on the floor.

The force of the fall knocked much of the rust off, so he repeated the process over and over until it started to look like a rail—albeit, a heavily rusted rail.

He then sat down on one of his board-dams and began tugging on the rail, trying to drag it away from the pile.

It was much heavier than he'd anticipated. Even with large scabs of the metal oxidation chipping off as muddied rust, the rail still weighed more than he did.

Red diligently toiled until he had freed up a total of four ten-foot rails—for what use they might be for his escape he did not yet know.

Even though the temperature was in the fifties, because of the humidity and his enormous exertion, he started sweating. Perspiration mixed with mud began streaking his face and running into his eyes and mouth.

He could only imagine Kate's vexation were she to see him now—her whole box of wipes would barely make a dent.

He smiled, thinking of her and what a great big sister/mom she was becoming.

He then turned back to the debris pile to see what useful objects he might find there. Holding the cell phone close to the backfilled debris, he slowly made his way from one side of the shaft to the other.

Finally, he ran across something that looked interesting. Almost in the middle, he saw a few links of a chain draped across the top of the coal car. Pulling off several stones and chunks of decayed wood exposed a chain running all the way to the floor. He followed it upward with the light, and he saw that it ran through a pulley assembly that was attached to a very thick beam spanning the entire roof.

"That looks like a block and tackle!" he muttered as only he could mutter. Exerting a series of sharp tugs on the chain, he managed to free up the pulleys.

Not only had he discovered a block and tackle, but it appeared to be an *operational* block and tackle. Because it was located in an area that was not susceptible to direct contact with water, it looked to be in relatively good condition.

He figured that looters had left it there after they were finished pillaging everything of value left behind by the original miners.

When a mine is closed, virtually all the equipment is left in place, as it is deemed easier and cheaper to replace it with new than it would be to remove it. Additionally, the harsh environment of a mine takes such a toll on the equipment that it's not prudent to reuse it.

That's why abandoned mines provide looters with a treasure trove of salvageable objects—their only challenge to cashing in is the struggle of bringing their prizes to the surface. That was the purpose of the block and tackle.

As soon as he had convinced himself that the hoist was reasonably safe, he hooked the chain to one end of a rail by wrapping it around it several times. The heavy oxidation on the rail allowed the chain to dig into it. He was easily able to lift the entire rail off the floor. He pushed the bottom of the vertical shaft of steel to within two feet of the wall. Once the bottom was resting on the floor, but before he took any more tension off the hoist, he shoved the top of the rail toward the wall and then lowered it rapidly.

He repeated this process until all four rails were upright and leaning against the wall. Red pointed his light at the tops of the rails. They were closer to the roof but still not close enough.

He then took a long look at the hoist again and smiled. "*That* just might work," he mumbled. "At least it would be worth a try."

Chapter 62
The missing cell phone

"Pull over up here," Glenda barked. "I've got to find my cell phone. What if I lost it in the woods out by where we left the boys? If someone were to find it there, they could trace it back to us."

"Back to *us*, eh?" Jeremy mocked.

"Face it," Glenda retorted. "If they catch either one of us, they will make a case against *both*."

"When's the last time you used your cell?" Jeremy asked, pulling the Marlboro pack out from his left front pocket and pushing in the lighter.

"I don't think I've used it all day," she said. "But do I recall switching it to my jacket pocket just before we started tossing those boards into the shaft. It's possible that I dropped it somewhere around the old mine. I suppose I might have even dropped it *into* the shaft when we were adjusting the boards. I just don't know where I might have dropped it."

"When the Handlers come to pick them up," he said, "if they run into us out there, it will not be a good thing. And you can be sure that they will find the bikes—"

"Unless we move them first," she interrupted.

Glenda continued to search for her phone while Jeremy pulled off on North Point Road. He parked on the shoulder, and both he and Glenda opened up the back of the trailer and searched it thoroughly for the phone. But they had no luck.

"What if we turn around and head back toward Hiawatha?" he suggested. "If we get stopped again I can tell the officer that we had just been stopped for the same thing and we decided that it would be too dangerous to continue on to Houghton, so we returned to drop off the trailer. We can leave it at Valley Spur. It's a trailhead for mountain biking. We won't be the only trailer dropped off there.

"We can run the Gators back to where the boys left their bikes, cut the locks off, and we can toss them in the back of a Gator. Then we will go find your phone. Shouldn't take long. And then reload the Gators on the trailer.

"I think we should then leave the trailer there until we can come back with a truck to pick it up. Maybe come back even tonight."

At first Glenda did not respond to his suggestions. She was stewing. In almost every other instance, she could find some way to lay all the blame for a mistake onto Jeremy, whom she generally thought to be worthless—but not this time.

As best she could recall, Jeremy never even touched her cell phone. She alone was responsible for having lost it. So, because she could not legitimately criticize him, even though she did not want to leave the trailer anywhere near Valley Spur, she simply sat staring straight ahead, silently boiling in anger and frustration.

Jeremy took her silence for agreement and headed back to Valley Spur.

Chapter 63

How long before we pick them up?

As planned, Jack and Kate left Sugar Island in the early afternoon and headed straight for the Christmas casino, just west of Munising. The drive took them two and a half hours.

Just as they were about to turn into the Kewadin parking lot, they were forced to wait for an unusually long motorhome pulling a large enclosed trailer.

"How'd you like to be piloting that around here in January?" Kate asked.

"That's got to be pushing the legal limit," Jack responded. "Pea soup, you say?"

"*Split*-pea soup," she corrected him. "You're gonna love it."

"I'll bet they have good hamburgers, too," Jack said. "I've heard that these casinos have some of the best food around. By the way, have you heard from the boys at all today?"

"I haven't talked to them since we dropped them off," Kate said. "I've tried to call them a few times, but if they don't have service, they would turn their phones off to save battery."

"It'd been nice if they would have tried to call us, to give us specific info on times and places for the pickup. I guess we can just assume that we should pick them up at dusk, at Valley Spur, if we don't hear differently."

"I think it's all we can do," she agreed.

"I would like to get to Valley Spur at around five—no later. We can entertain ourselves until they get there."

"That means," Kate said, "that means we should leave the casino at four-thirty. That should give us just enough time to eat and use the restroom."

"So, it's the wrong day of the week for pea soup," Jack said as he checked out the menu. "I'm *really* disappointed. I suppose I'll just have to order a burger, and maybe a shake."

Kate attempted once more to call the boys—first she tried Red's phone and then Robby's. But she didn't get through.

"No luck?" Jack asked as he took a bite of his bison burger, genuinely relieved that this was not pea-soup day at the casino.

Kate had opted for the salad bar with a Diet Coke and the soup of the day, which was wild rice chicken.

"No. But that's not surprising. If they left their phones on at all out there, it would have run their batteries down. Even if they have made their way back to Valley Spur, they might not have enough battery to make or receive a call. We're just going to have to go there and find out."

"Exactly," Jack said. "It doesn't mean a thing—that we can't reach them. They're probably already there waiting for us, cold and hungry."

"Probably freezing their tails off," Kate followed.

Just before leaving, Kate summoned the waitress.

"Stick two burgers just like my dad had in a to-go bag, please. Actually, make it three—can't forget about Buddy. Skip the shake, but add a couple hot chocolates."

Chapter 64

It'll be a cold day in hell

After about ten minutes, she finally broke her silence. "We're not going to leave *anything* at Valley Spur. We've got bolt cutters with us—right? We'll pick up the bikes, find the phone, and then we'll go back to Houghton. It'll be a cold day in hell before I ever come back to this area."

Neither of them spoke another word until they had parked in the far southeast corner of the Valley Spur parking area.

Glenda opened the back of the trailer and dropped the ramp. As soon as she had unloaded one Gator, she barked, "We'll only need one. Get in. I'll drive.

"Do you have the bolt cutters?"

"No, but I do have a DeWalt high-speed grinder. Bolt cutters won't touch those locks," Jeremy said with a bit of a "back atcha" tone. He held it up a little too close to her face and then tossed it on the floorboard between them.

"Won't that start a fire?"

"It could, but bolt cutters won't work on locks like those. We'll just have to be careful."

"We should get the bikes *first*," she said. "And then we'll go in and look for the cell."

"Exactly."

They shot into the forest and past the gate where the bikes were secured, skidding to a stop behind a larger tree. Cutting the locks with the high-speed grinder was a snap. They then tossed the bikes into the back of the Gator and covered them up.

"When we get close to the mine," she ordered, "I will park the Gator, and we will walk the rest of the way. No point in leaving tire tracks leading up to the mine. Just be sure you bring the rope ladder, shovels, and flashlights. Let's make this quick."

They parked the ORV just as planned and walked over to the mineshaft.

"You remember having the phone *at* the mine?" he asked.

"That's what I already told you!" she bit back at him.

They spent ten minutes searching the area surrounding the mine's opening. And even though they were not speaking loudly, Red heard them.

Chapter 65

We're gonna have to open it up

Jeremy and Glenda spent close to twenty minutes searching the area around the mineshaft.

Finally, Jeremy pulled his cell out of his right-hand pants pocket and declared, "I've got service! Right here. Right where I'm standing at this second, I've got service. I'm gonna call your phone before it goes away."

"My phone is on vibrate," Glenda said. "But we should be able to hear it if we listen closely."

"It went immediately to voicemail," Jeremy said. "I'll try it again."

He did, and again his call went to her voicemail.

"That means wherever my phone is, it's either broken, the battery is discharged, or it does not have service. I think it's doubtful that it's broken or discharged. So it's probably right under this roof opening, *inside* the mine. We've got to find it."

They decided to shovel the leaves and topsoil to one side of the roof. Once they had a strip a few feet wide cleared off from one side to the other, they would find a seam in the tarpaper and roll it back to expose the boards.

They had not nailed the tarpaper or the boards, so their task was not a difficult one. Jeremy positioned himself on one end, Glenda on the other. Carefully they lifted four planks off the roof and stacked them to the side.

"Okay," she said. "That should do it. *If* it fell in, it should be directly beneath this opening."

Glenda began shining her flashlight around the floor of the mine.

"Oh my God!" she exclaimed. "Somebody's been really busy down there. The whole floor is covered with tracks. One of the boys must *not* have slid all the way down the incline. At least not right away. They're not around now. Must be one of them managed to make it back up to the top. That couldn't have been easy."

"And look right there," Jeremy said. "Doesn't that look like your phone?"

She shined her flashlight over where Jeremy was looking.

"It sure is," she declared. "I guess I did drop it in there after all. Tie that ladder onto a tree and drop it through the hole. We need to get that phone and get outta here."

Jeremy did as he was told, but before he began his descent, he saw one of the rails lying on the floor with a chain wrapped around it.

"What the hell went on down there?" he said. "I don't recall seeing that chain before."

"Just go down there and get the damn phone! They're only kids. And they're not even around. They must have slid on down the incline. Just get the damn phone so we can get *outta* here!"

Jeremy was used to taking orders from her. So in his well-practiced, dutiful manner he turned around at the ladder and lowered himself into the mine until his feet found the rungs so that he could support his weight for the descent.

Just as his eyes passed the bottom of the roof he spotted Red's terrified face.

Because Red had heard them talking about the phone, he had placed it back where he had found it on the floor.

He'd then used the hoist to lift himself as high as he could manage. He'd found that once he had pulled himself up, he couldn't maintain his position without constantly pulling on the haul chain. So he'd wrapped the haul around his foot to maintain height and reached over until he could pull one of the rails toward him.

He had then wrapped the haul chain several times around the rail and pushed the heavy piece of steel away from him. Not only had the weight of the rail kept the chain taut, but it had propelled him to the very top of the hoist.

And once the steel rail had fallen to within five feet of the floor, its weight exerted sufficient force on the haul chain to keep him at roof level.

When Jeremy saw Red, it so startled him that his right foot slipped through the rope ladder, causing him to lose his balance and fall backward.

"Oh my God!" he screamed over and over. "Help me!"

Glenda did not know that Red was tucked in just beneath the bottom of the roof. When she reached down to help Jeremy, she also spotted Red.

"What the hell are you doing up there?" she screamed at him.

She leaned farther over the edge to get a better look at just how Red was suspending himself at the roof and to survey Jeremy's predicament.

Chapter 66
Going down

She would have been fine had Jeremy not panicked. He was hanging on the rope ladder by only one knee, and the 1¼-inch aluminum rung was cutting off circulation to the rest of his right leg and foot.

As soon as he saw her leaning over close to him, he used his last bit of energy to reach out to her. Bending at the waist, he lunged forward just far enough to grab her arm.

It was a foolish move on his part. For starters, he outweighed her by more than eighty pounds. His fingers gripped her forearm like a vice at the apex of his ill-fated maneuver. And then, when he began to collapse back down, his momentum pulled her off the roof and down into the mineshaft.

As soon as Jeremy realized what he had done, he released his grip. But it was too late.

She grabbed at Jeremy's shirt as she fell past him. Of course, it was not enough to stop her fall—his buttons gave way, but her fall was not broken.

The short moment that she was able to hold onto his shirt was enough to prevent her from crashing into the floor face first. Instead, she landed on both feet, twenty degrees off vertical. The initial impact, while absorbing much of the force of the fall, shattered both of her ankles.

Glenda's screams continued until the back of her head smacked heavily onto the floor.

When Jeremy looked down, even though blood was pooling in his head, distorting his vision, and even though his girlfriend had fallen mostly outside the area illuminated through the opening they had just made in the roof of the mine, his eyes soon found her outstretched form.

Despite enormous pressure behind his eyes, Jeremy forced them to focus on her face. She had finally come to rest on her back, with most of her body concealed by the blackness of the upside shadows—only her face lay outside the darkness.

Her gaping mouth seemed caught mid-scream by the fall. Her unblinking eyes stared directly at Jeremy, and a small rivulet of blood had begun to seep down the incline.

Jeremy knew she was dying. But he was not quite sure why. He grew still as his mind raced to make sense of it.

I don't get it, he reasoned. *Her legs should have broken the fall. The bump on the head should not have killed her.*

Jeremy did not realize that the soft tissue on the back of her head had found the curved end of the rod Red had been using. While penetration was not great, it was enough to puncture and destroy her brainstem.

Her heart continued to beat for only a few seconds, causing the stream of blood to stop before it reached the shadows on the downward side of the incline. She was dead.

The shock was too great for Jeremy. He could not bear to think about continuing to live without her.

In a conscious effort to join her on the floor in death, he straightened the leg that was wrapped around the rung of the ladder. But, even in this effort, he failed.

As his calf slid along the rung, his sizeable shoe caught in the rung above, and his whole foot became inextricably entangled in the ropes of the ladder. No matter how hard he tried, he could not free it enough to fall.

Red waited until Jeremy's body grew still, and then he went to work.

The ladder was almost within Red's reach. He was sure that if he leaned toward it and let loose of the block and tackle, that he could grab it on his descent.

He would have liked to wait longer, because he was not certain about the condition of the man hanging upside down only a few feet away.

Red didn't think that the man was faking unconsciousness, but he wasn't certain.

Robby needs me to get help, he thought. *I've gotta make my move. And I've gotta do it now.*

Red leaned as far as he could and then attempted to kick off against the block and tackle. But, instead of his being able to exert force against it, the pulley assembly shot backward. Red fell downward like a limp doll.

Fortunately, however, even this minimal trajectory carried him close enough to the ladder to grasp it on his way down.

But while he had hoped to grab onto the ladder directly above the man, he unfortunately ended up well down the ladder—one rung past Jeremy's head.

The sudden jolt on the ladder caused the man to stir. Opening his eyes, he thrust his hands toward Red, locking the fingers of his left hand into Red's long curly hair and clutching Red's right wrist with his other hand.

"You bastard!" he exclaimed, as he tried to yank Red off the ladder. "You *killed* her!"

Chapter 67

It did not look right to Kate

Jack and Kate were just arriving at Valley Spur. Kate continued her efforts to call Red and Robby as they pulled into the parking lot off M-94.

"You're worried about them?" Jack asked.

"A little," she replied, looking at her watch. "They have over an hour before dusk, but I would be much happier if I were able to get through to them. Doesn't it seem like they should have touched base with us before this? It's been almost two full days."

"It would have been nice," Jack said. "But, when I was their age, the last thing I would have wanted to do would be to *encourage* adult interference. I can appreciate their desire for independence. But I would agree—it would have made it more pleasant for *us* if they had reached out a little better."

"Take a look at that," Kate said, pointing at the motorhome

parked in the corner of the parking lot. "That looks a *lot* like the one we saw on 28, when we were pulling into the casino. And check *that* out. The driver side door is wide open. And the ramp is still attached. That looks *very* weird to me."

"Sure does look strange," Jack agreed.

So, instead of parking in a fashion that would allow him to keep an eye out for Red and Robby coming across M-94 (where he anticipated they would emerge from the forest), he pulled right up beside the open door of the motor home.

"You check the outside, and I'll hit the inside," he said.

Kate didn't reply. Instead, as soon as Jack had stopped, she shot out of his SUV and headed straight for the back of the trailer.

The padlock is in the hasp, but not locked, she was thinking. *I wonder what's inside.*

Carefully she opened up the rear doors, making sure that there was no one with bad intentions lying in wait.

"What the hell!" she muttered, spotting the Gator.

"That ATV has to be worth at least ten grand," she said aloud. "That just doesn't make any sense."

She then closed the doors back up and continued on around to the front passenger door. She found it locked, so she continued around to the open driver-side door. Jack was sitting in the driver's seat.

"Take a look at this," he said, handing her some papers. "Anything grab your attention?"

Kate received the documents her father was handing her and studied them for only a moment.

"That last name, *Henry*. That's the same as that professor—Dr. Wilbur Henry."

"It sure is," Jack replied. "And check out where it was leased—Houghton. That's got to be more than a coincidence. I'd be willing to bet that this Glenda Henry is the professor's wife, or spinster sister. What did you find in the trailer?"

"There's one Gator back there," Kate replied, "and it looks like one's missing."

"And the ramp is down," Jack said. "Let's take a look."

The two of them raced back to the ramp and examined the tracks carefully.

"Looks like there were two of them—a man and a woman. They backed one down the ramp," Jack said, carefully scrutinizing the tracks the Gator left. "And here, a female jumped up on the ramp and closed the doors. But she did not take the time to lock it up?"

"And it looks like she was driving," Kate said.

"Plus they left the driver's door of the motorhome wide open," Jack added. "They were in one big hurry to do something."

Jack took a long look at the remaining Gator and then ran up the ramp. Ten seconds later he had it running and was backing it off the trailer.

"Jump in," he shouted, as he hit the remote to lock his Tahoe.

"Is this auto theft?" Kate asked.

"It could be grand theft auto for all I care," Jack muttered. "I don't give a damn. What the hell county is this, anyway? Alger? Is this *Alger* County? Looks like I'm gonna get to meet a new sheriff. Snug up that seatbelt, Kitty, this is gonna be a rough ride."

Jack was angry. He didn't talk much as the two of them shot across M-94 and headed west on Buck Bay Road.

"Looks like these guys knew *exactly* where they were going,"

Jack said. "Check out the tracks they left us. They didn't even try to cover them up."

Kate knew what he was thinking, and she agreed. Both she and her father initially suspected that Professor Henry was somehow involved in the murder of Robby's parents, as well as the crew members of his father's boat, the *Snoopy*. But when it became clear that Dr. Henry could not personally have been responsible for the murders, the case just seemed to grow cold.

Neither of them suspected the professor's wife, Glenda Henry. And now, for some reason, Glenda Henry was knocking around in the same Hiawatha National Forest as Red and Robby were.

It just did not have the feel of a coincidental occurrence—not to Jack and not to Kate.

The tracks were easy to follow. The treads on the Gator were pronounced, and there had been no vehicles on Buck Bay Road after the first Gator.

When Jack and Kate reached the point where Buck Bay Road turns right, they saw that the first Gator had gone straight on USFS 2482, also known as 531.

Jack never slowed down as he shot past the intersection. A little more than two miles later he slammed on the brakes and then backed up.

"They took to the woods right here," he said, pointing to the tracks leading off to the right.

"They stopped there," Kate said. "Look at those tracks. What were they doing?"

"Sit tight," Jack commanded as he jumped out and ran over to the spot Kate was talking about. He reached down and picked something up and then jumped back behind the steering wheel.

"Take a look at this," he said, handing Kate what remained of one of the locks the boys had used to secure their bikes.

Kate was deeply worried. For one thing, she was fearful of what they might find. *Are the boys okay*? She wondered. *Or has this woman harmed them like it appears she did Robby's parents?*

Kate acknowledged that she had no control over what had *already* taken place. But if the boys were still alive, she believed that the odds were good that she and her father would keep them alive.

But Kate had another concern. She was worried about what Jack would do to this Henry woman, and her friend, when he caught up to them. She strongly suspected her father would see to it that they never went to trial. And she did not want to witness it.

Kate was now convinced that it was only a matter of minutes, or perhaps seconds, before they would reach the boys. She was right.

Jack did not say anything when he spotted the other Gator. He simply pointed at it to make sure Kate had also seen it.

Kate then took off her seatbelt and stood up to get a better view of the terrain. She grabbed the roll bar with both hands to stabilize herself.

"There!" she shouted. "Something's been going on over there!" She was pointing at a pile of roof boards from the mine's opening.

Jack pulled up to within inches and slammed on his brakes.

Chapter 68

Jack drew his gun

Jack drew his Smith and Wesson .38 Special and carefully peered over the edge of the roof. He did not like what he saw. He motioned for Kate to stand back.

As his eyes adjusted to the darkness, the first thing he spotted was the body of an adult male hanging by one foot from a rope ladder. By the way the man was hanging, he knew he was dead—one foot was caught up in the ladder, one leg bent at the knee and dangling to the side of the man's body, and both of his arms hanging downward.

"The man is dead," he announced to Kate. "I can't see the woman."

Leaning farther into the darkness so that his eyes could better adjust, he finally spotted the body of the woman.

"She's dead too," he said. "I'm pretty sure there were only two of them. And they're both dead. Take a look down here and see what you think. I don't see the boys anywhere around."

Kate leaned over to take a look as Jack holstered his gun.

"Red, Robby, can you hear me?" Kate yelled as loudly as she could.

Buddy whined.

"I heard Buddy," she said. "I'm goin' in."

Kate did not wait for her father's okay. She grasped the topmost rung of the ladder and threw her feet into the darkness. When her foot struck Jeremy's, she reached around the ladder, suspended her weight with her hands, and continued down on the reverse side of the ladder.

"Careful this guy doesn't dislodge and fall on you," Jack said as she reached the bottom.

Jack then followed. When he reached the tangled foot, he checked to see where Kate was standing and then simply hooked his foot under the dead man's and lifted. That freed the body to fall in a heap next to Glenda's.

Kate took her cell out of her pocket and activated the flash-light.

"I see them!" she shouted. "Red seems to be okay, but Robby isn't moving."

By the time Jack had reached the bottom of the ladder, Kate had used the labyrinth of boards Red had made to lower herself to where Red and Robby were.

Red was sitting on the incline, legs braced to keep him from sliding into the water, with Robby's head cradled in his arms.

When Kate shone her light on them, Red did his best to wipe the tears from his eyes. He did not want Kate to see him crying.

"How is he?" Kate asked.

Red had just seen two people die in front of him. He knew Robby was badly injured, and he feared the worst. Red did not respond to Kate's question. He simply burst out crying, and this time he did not try to hide it.

"Here, darlin'," Kate said, sliding closer to the two boys. "Let me get a closer look."

Kate reached under Robby's arms and pulled him over to where she could examine his injury.

"Just his head? As far as you know?" she asked.

Red nodded.

"Has he moved or tried to talk since he bumped it?"

At first Red shook his head, and then he caught himself. Enunciating a small grunt, he then nodded in the affirmative.

Kate thought for a moment and then asked, "He was okay at first, and then he went unconscious?"

Red nodded.

Kate felt his neck.

"Your friend is alive," she said. "He's got a very strong heartbeat. That's good. But we do need to get him to a hospital."

"Dad, Robby needs help," she called up to her father. "Do you have any service down here?"

"No," he replied without checking. "Can you get him up here?"

"Yeah," she said.

"You get him up here, and I'll carry him up the ladder."

Kate reached up the incline with her left hand until she could securely dig her fingers into the top of the next board-dam.

With her right arm wrapped around Robby's chest, she prepared to pull herself and the boy up to the next level. Red had already gone ahead and was reaching down to help. But before she made the move, she called up to her father.

"Dad, call Buddy," she said. "We need to make sure he gets to the top before we start up."

"Hey. Buddy," Jack called. "Get up here."

Buddy complied with the command, using each board-dam to launch himself to the next.

Once the dog was safe, Kate gave an order to Red, who had taken a secure position directly above her.

"As soon as you can reach him," she said, "grab onto Robby's shirt and help me pull him up."

Red nodded his head. Even though Kate could not see his response, she knew that he was ready to help.

Kate placed her feet on the apex of the first board-dam and thrust Robby up toward Red. As soon as he could reach his friend, Red gripped Robby by the shirt and helped lift him to the next level.

And so the process unfolded. Kate would lift Robby as far up the incline as she could, and then Red would help her secure the injured boy on the boards above.

Together they conquered the board-dams, one after another.

Finally, Kate reached the point where her father could help. He grabbed her by the collar and pulled her and Robby the rest of the way up.

Jack wasted no time. He tossed Robby over his shoulder and headed toward the rope ladder.

But before he was able to start, Red let out one of his patented growls. Jack knew that Red intended it to get his attention.

"Son, what's up?"

Red reached into his pocket and removed the piece of metal he had found on the mine floor and had used to scratch the hour lines on the floor. He handed it to Jack.

"What have we got here?" Jack said through a giant smile. "Well, I'll be damned! Robby is going to love this."

Red had handed his uncle a perfectly formed Bronze Age spearhead.

Red's eyes met Jack's, and with his free hand Jack drew Red to him and hugged him tightly.

Kate watched them until they reached the top. Once at the top, Jack turned and spoke to Kate. "We've gotta get Robby some help. And quickly. I fear that this could be more than just a concussion. It's possible that his brain is swelling. I'm going to lay Robby in the Gator and see if I can get service on my cell. As soon as I can make a call, I'll make arrangements to get an ambulance. Can you wrap it up here?"

"We'll figure something out," Kate said. "You just concentrate on Robby."

As soon as Jack and Robby disappeared, Kate turned to Red and said, "Got any ideas on how we're going to get Buddy out of here?"

He motioned for Kate to go up the ladder first. As soon as she reached the top, Red untangled the rail from the block and tackle chain and lowered it to the floor. He then removed his shirt and belt and constructed a harness for Buddy.

Buddy did not think much of the makeshift device, but he trusted Red.

After he had determined that it would be strong enough to support Buddy, he hooked it to the block and tackle and elevated his trusting friend to the top of the mine and then secured the chain to the rail on the floor.

Red then climbed up the rope ladder to where Buddy was suspended. Placing Buddy's front paws on his shoulder, he unhooked the harness and lifted Buddy to Kate's waiting arms.

Chapter 69
Sheriff Green, I could use some help

Sheriff, Jack Handler here. Do you suppose you could meet me at the hospital in Munising?"

"What have you broken now?" Sheriff Green asked. "I trust this is very important. I'm sure you know that is out of my jurisdiction."

"It's important all right," Jack replied. "Red and Robby just cracked the rest of your big murder case."

"What! What are you saying?" Sheriff Green asked. "What *exactly* are you trying to tell me?"

"They just solved the murder of Robby's mother," Jack said. "And, you might want to notify your buddy over there in Luce that the boys solved his Little Lake Harbor murders as well. Those nine killings are his responsibility. I'm sure he'll be eager to hear about it."

"Are you sure about this?" Sheriff Green asked in disbelief.

"Oh yeah," Jack chuckled. "We're sure."

"And let me guess—the killers are dead?" Sheriff Green asked. "They are. Right, Jack? The killers are all dead?"

"Well, two of them are," Jack replied. "I'm pretty sure there's one more, and I suspect his name is Art. I've got a phone number for him. Took it off the phone belonging to a woman named Glenda Henry.

"But all the good guys are alive. I guess you couldn't say 'alive and *well*.' Robby took a pretty good knock to the head, but he's coming around. Doctors say he'll be just fine. Oh, to be young and healthy. If I'd taken a bump on my head like he did, they'd be calling the undertaker. Anyway, the doctor wants to keep him a day or so for observation. But, other than that, everybody else, at least the ones that matter, are just fine."

"Did you say Glenda Henry?" the sheriff asked.

"Exactly. Remember Professor Henry?" Jack asked.

"Really?" the sheriff asked, sounding surprised. "I thought we ruled him out."

"It wasn't him. It was his wife and her boyfriend," Jack said. "They were professors at the same college."

"Motive?" the sheriff asked. "Did they have a motive?"

"What it comes down to is this," Jack replied. "Had Titus Gordon been able to substantiate his theory about the Minoan copper ship having its origin in the Bronze Age, it would have turned early American history on its head. They committed the murders to protect their theory—their body of work. How totally self-absorbed. They're supposed to be *educators*, and they turned out to be nothing but charlatans."

"And we thought Dr. Henry was the bad apple," the sheriff added.

"Well," Jack said. "He still might turn out to be as *intellectually* corrupt as his wife and her friend, but he's not your killer."

"It's going to take me a few minutes to get outta here," the sheriff said. "But as soon as I do I'll head west."

"Whatcha got going on that's so important?" Jack asked. It seemed a little strange to him that the sheriff would not drop everything and head that way. After all, there was going to be a lot of glory dished out, and elected officials generally want all the good publicity they can get.

"I'm just mopping up on a suicide," the sheriff said. "Strangest thing. This guy gets in from Chicago … just a few hours ago. And he overdoses at his hotel right here in the Soo."

"From *Chicago*?" Jack inquired.

"Right."

"Do you have a name?" Jack asked.

"He checked in as Dmitri Black," the sheriff said. "But we ran his prints, and we came up with a *Reginald* Black—no middle name. But he apparently has roots, or at least some history, in Chicago."

Jack could not speak.

Suddenly the sheriff realized what had just happened. "Oh my God! Jack. Could this Reginald Black, could he be your friend? Reg?"

Jack did not respond immediately. Even though he did not confirm the dead man's identity as his friend, the sheriff understood that it was.

"Jack, I am so sorry for your loss. I'll get over there as quickly as I can."

"Good. That would be good," Jack said. "See you in a bit."

Jack stood motionless—his exhilaration at having concluded a difficult case turned to deep sadness.

He reached into his pocket and pulled out his wallet. Carefully he removed a small piece of bloodied paper and unfolded it.

Pressing it against the wall and staring at and past it, he muttered, "Well, old friend. Is the solution of your puzzle going to die with you this time?"

The Inscrutable Puzzle?

In *Jack and the New York Death Mask* (first book in the "Getting to Know Jack" series) Jack's close friend, Reginald (Reg) Black, left this bloody cryptogram for Jack to find when he (Reg) was shot in a successful attempt to free Kate (Jack's daughter) from her Eastern European abductors.

At the time he discovered it (in Reg's blood-soaked trousers) Jack knew it was significant, and that Reg had intended it for him to find. However, the first night that it was in his possession it was stolen from Jack's apartment. The culprits: two of former First Lady Allison Fulbright's operatives. Fortunately, Jack had copied the puzzle and had taken an image of it before the theft.

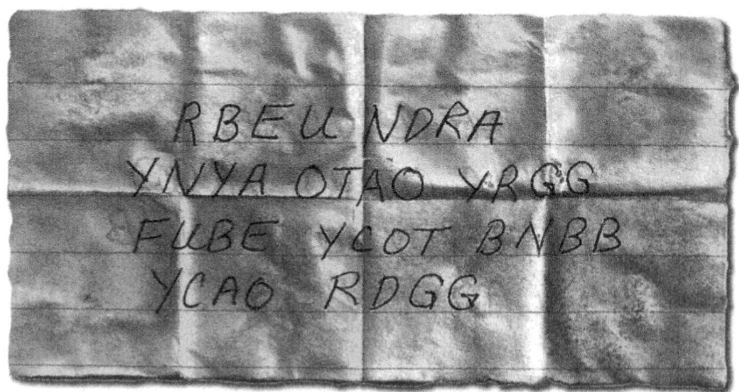
RBEU NDRA
YNYA OTAO YRGG
FUBE YCOT BNBB
YCAO RDGG

Now Allison is reentering the picture. She wants to Exhume Reg's body from Calvary Cemetery in Queens, New York. Jack does not know her motivation, nor does Pam Black, Reg's widow.

Could it have something to do with the plaintext behind this cryptogram?

So far no one has been able to decipher the puzzle. Could it point to the location that Reg hid the one hundred million dollars in gold that he had received from Allison as payment for the assassination of a sitting president? Is that why Allison is so adamant about digging Reg up? As of right now, we don't know.

Some smart people have declared this puzzle to be inscrutable—unsolvable. But, we know better than that. There is no such thing as an unsolvable puzzle.

There is a key (of sorts) included with the puzzle in *Jack and the New York Death Mask.*

As this book unfolds, Reg's inscrutable puzzle remains just that—inscrutable. And Allison has not yet been satisfied.

Cast of Characters
in the Getting to Know Jack Series

If you want to find out more about the series, then I would encourage you to check out the publisher's website (http://www.greenwichvillageink.com).

Jack: Jack is a good man, in his way. While it is true that he kills a lot of people, it can be argued that most (if not all) of them needed killing. Occasionally a somewhat sympathetic figure comes between Jack and his goal. When that happens, Jack's goal comes first. I think the word that best sums up Jack's persona might be "expeditor." He is outcome driven—he makes things turn out the way he wants them to turn out.

For instance, if you were a single mom and a bully were stealing your kid's lunch money, you could send "Uncle Jack" to school with little Billy. Uncle Jack would have a talk with the teachers and the principal. With Jack's help, the problem would be solved. But I would not recommend that you ask him how he accomplished it. You might not like what he tells you—if he even responds.

Jack is faithful to his friends and a great father to his daughter. He is also a dangerous and tenacious adversary when situations require it.

To some extent, I look to the memory of my father in determining what Jack might do in certain situations. While my father did not make a habit of killing people, like Jack, my dad was tough. From the age of thirteen my father was on his own. Working in Newberry (in Upper Michigan) as a lumberjack, he always carried a sidearm. It came in handy because he was also the area's moonshiner.

But even given his hard life, I never knew my father to lie, cheat, or act in any dishonorable fashion. He was a great father and friend. Jack is like that.

Jack Handler began his career as a law enforcement officer. He married a beautiful woman of Greek descent (Beth) while working as a police officer in Chicago. She was a concert violinist and the love of his life. If you were to ask Jack about it, he would quickly tell you he married above himself. So when she was killed by bullets intended for him, he admittedly grew bitter. Kate, their daughter, was barely a year old when her mother was gunned down.

As a single father trying to raise a daughter on his own, Jack soon found that he needed to make more money than his job paid. So he went back to college and got a degree in criminal justice. Soon he was promoted to the level of sergeant in the Chicago Police Homicide Division.

With the help of a friend, he then discovered that there was much more money to be earned in the private sector. At first he began moonlighting on private security jobs. Immediate success led him to take an early retirement and obtain his private investigator license.

Because of his special talents (obtained as a former Army Ranger) and his intense dedication to problem solving, many of Jack's jobs emerged from the darker side. While Jack did take on some of the more sketchy clients, he never accepted a project simply on the basis of financial gain—he always sought out the moral high ground. Unfortunately, all too often that moral high ground morphed into quicksand.

Jack is now pushing sixty, and he has all the physical problems common to a man that age. While it is true that he remains in amazing physical condition, of late he has begun to sense his limitations.

His biggest concern right now, however, is an impending IRS audit. He isn't totally confident that it will turn out okay.

His problems stem from the purchase of half-interest in a bar in Chicago nearly two decades earlier. His partner was one of his oldest and most trusted friends.

The principal reason he made the investment was to create a cover for his private security business.

Many, if not most, of his clients insisted on paying him in cash or with some other untraceable commodity. At first he tried getting rid of the cash by paying all of his bills with it. But even though he meticulously avoided credit cards and checks, the cash continued to accumulate.

It wasn't that he was in any sense averse to paying his fair share of taxes. The problem was that if he did deposit the cash into a checking account, and subsequently included it in his filings, he would then at some point be required to explain where it had come from.

He needed an acceptable method of laundering, and his buddy's bar seemed perfect.

But it did not work out as planned. Almost one year ago the IRS decided to audit the bar.

Jack hired one of his old customers, a disbarred attorney/CPA, to see if this shady character could get the books straightened out enough for Jack to survive the audit and avoid federal prison.

The accountant knew exactly how Jack earned his money and that the sale of a few bottles of Jack Daniels had little to do with it.

Even though his business partner and the CPA talked a good game about legitimacy, Jack still agonized about it when such thoughts barged through his mind.

Reg: In *Jack and the New York Death Mask (Death Mask)* Jack is recruited by his best friend, Reg (Reginald Black), to do a job without either man having any knowledge as to what that job might entail. Jack, out of loyalty to his friend, accepted the offer. The contract was ostensibly to assassinate a sitting president. However, instead of assisting the plot, Jack and Reg worked to thwart it. Most of this story takes place in New York City, but there are scenes in DC, Chicago, and Upstate New York. Reg is frequently mentioned throughout the series, as are Pam Black and Allison Fulbright. Pam Black is Reg's wife (he was shot at the end of *Death Mask*), and Allison is a former first lady. It was Allison who contracted Reg and Jack to assassinate the sitting president. She is currently on Pam Black's case, trying to get back the money she had paid Reg in the failed assassination scheme. Also, she still has aspirations on being president.

Kate: Kate, Jack's daughter and a New York homicide detective, is introduced early in this book. Kate is beautiful. She has her mother's olive complexion and green eyes. Her trim five-foot-eight frame, with her long auburn hair falling nicely on her broad shoulders, would seem more at home on the runway than in an interrogation room. But Kate is a seasoned New York homicide detective. In fact, she is thought by many to be on the fast track to the top—thanks in part to the unwavering support of her soon-to-retire boss, Captain Spencer.

Of course, her career was not hindered by her background in law. Graduating summa cum laude from Notre Dame at the age of twenty-one, she went on to Notre Dame Law School. She passed the Illinois Bar Exam immediately upon receiving her JD, and accepted a position at one of Chicago's most prestigious criminal law firms. While her future looked bright as a courtroom attorney, she hated defending "sleazebags."

One Saturday morning she called her father and invited him to meet her at what she knew to be his favorite coffee house. It was there, over a couple espressos, that she asked him what he thought about her taking a position with the New York Police Department. She was shocked when he immediately gave his blessing. "Kitty," he said, "you're a smart girl. I totally trust your judgment. You have to go where your heart leads. Just promise me one thing. Guarantee me that you will put me up whenever I want to visit. After all, you are my favorite daughter."

To this Kate replied with a chuckle, "Dad, I'm your only daughter. And you will always be welcome."

In *Murder on Sugar Island (Sugar)*, Jack and Kate team up to solve the murder of Alex, Jack's brother-in-law. This book takes place on Sugar Island, which is located in the northern part of Michigan's Upper Peninsula (just east of Sault Ste. Marie, MI).

A new main character is introduced in this book: Red, a redheaded thirteen-year-old who, besides being orphaned, cannot speak.

One other character of significance introduced in this book is

Bill Green, the knowledgeable police officer who first appears in Joey's coffee shop. He assumes a major role in subsequent books of the series.

Red: Red has a number of outstanding characteristics—first of all, in his ability to take care of himself in all situations. When his parents were killed in a fire, Red chose to live on his own instead of submitting to placement in foster care.

During the warmer months, he lived in a hut he had pieced together from parts of abandoned homes, barns, and cottages, and he worked at a resort on Sugar Island. In the winter, he would take up residence in empty fishing cottages along the river.

Red's second outstanding characteristic is his loyalty. When put to the test, Red would rather sacrifice his life than see his friends hurt. In *Sugar,* Red works together with Jack and Kate to solve the mystery behind the killing of Jack's brother-in-law Alex. Alex was the owner of the resort where Red worked, and he shared a very significant relationship with the boy.

The third thing about Red that makes him stand out is his inability to speak. As the result of a traumatic event in his life, his voice box was damaged, resulting in his disability. Before Jack and Kate entered his life, Red communicated only through an improvised sign system, and various grunts.

When Kate introduced him to a cell phone, and texting, Red's life changed dramatically.

In *Superior Peril (Peril)* and *Superior Intrigue (Intrigue)* all of the above characters play major roles. Plus there were some new colorful characters introduced in these two books.